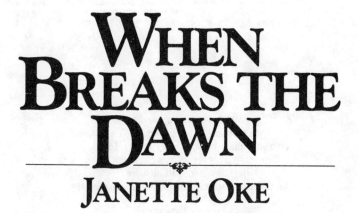

WHEN BREAKS THE DAWN

JANETTE OKE

JO

WHEN BREAKS THE DAWN
A Literary Express, Inc. Book
(a subsidiary of Doubleday Direct, Inc.)
Reprinted by special arrangement with:
Bethany House Publishers
A Ministry of Bethany Fellowship International

PRINTING HISTORY
A Bethany House Publication / April 1986
The Janette Oke Collection / 1997

If you would be interested in purchasing additional copies of this
book, or have any questions concerning the Janette Oke
Collection and your membership, or if you would like to
correspond with the author, please contact us at:

The Janette Oke Collection
Literary Express, Inc.
1540 Broadway
New York, NY 10036
Telephone #973-473-4800

ISBN: 1-58165-141-4

Printed in the United States of America

To my dear fifth sister, Joyce Ruth,
whom I had the privilege of
helping to name when she arrived
and to spoil as she grew.
I appreciate her unselfish love
and her dedication to her Lord.
To her and to her husband, Elmer Deal,
I dedicate this book with my love.

JANETTE OKE was born in Champion, Alberta, during the depression years, to a Canadian prairie farmer and his wife. She is a graduate of Mountain View Bible College in Didsbury, Alberta, where she met her husband, Edward. They were married in May of 1957, and went on to pastor churches in Indiana as well as Calgary and Edmonton, Canada.

The Okes have three sons and one daughter and are enjoying the addition to the family of grandchildren. Edward and Janette have both been active in their local church, serving in various capacities as Sunday-school teachers and board members. They make their home in Didsbury, Alberta.

Contents

Synopsis

When Comes the Spring

When Elizabeth Thatcher, the fashion-conscious young schoolteacher from Toronto, boarded the train for Calgary, it was with one purpose in mind. She was going to teach pioneer children in a country school. But Wynn Delaney, a member of the Royal North West Mounted Police, entered her life and changed all that.

After a wedding in Calgary and a brief honeymoon in Banff, the couple left for the North where Wynn had been posted to a remote Indian village. Elizabeth soon learned to love and respect the Indian people even though the adjustment was difficult.

Tragedy struck the village when the trading post burned to the ground. With it went the vital winter supplies of the people. Nimmie McLain, the trader's Indian wife, had become Elizabeth's best friend, so Nimmie was missed terribly when she and her husband went "out," back to civilization, to arrange for more supplies and the materials to build a new store.

Nimmie promised they would return in the spring. Elizabeth watched for that day with great anticipation and longing. Finally it came, and with the coming of the wagons came hope, renewed strength, and joy.

CHARACTERS

ELIZABETH THATCHER DELANEY—schoolteacher and wife of Wynn. Though raised in comfortable circumstances in the city of Toronto, she learned to live on little, without fuss or self-pity.

WYNN DELANEY—a member of the Royal North West Mounted Police who saw his occupation as a means of caring for others.

IAN AND NIMMIE MCLAIN—owner of the settlement trading post and his self-educated Indian wife.

JON, MARY, WILLIAM, SARAH, KATHLEEN, ELIZABETH—the brother of Elizabeth, his wife and family. Their home was in Calgary.

JULIE—Elizabeth's pretty and somewhat flighty younger sister, whom she loved dearly.

MATTHEW—Elizabeth's younger brother, raised in Toronto.

Chapter One

The Homecoming

The nearer we came to the rumbling wagons, the more my heart pounded. Frustrated with the wait, I wished I could just hoist my long, cumbersome skirts and break into a run, but I held my impatience in check. I wasn't sure how Wynn would feel about my impulsiveness, and I was quite sure there would be some puzzled expressions on the faces of our Indian neighbors.

They were so near and yet so far away, just dipping down over the last hills before our little village. I had missed Nimmie so much in the time she had been gone, and was anxious to see for myself that she was all right. I wanted to hug her close, to welcome her back. I wanted to talk, and talk—for hours and hours—and to hear all about the outside world and every little thing that had happened to her while she had been away from us.

I'm sure Wynn sensed my feelings. He reached for my hand and gave it a loving squeeze.

"It won't be long now," he said, trying to calm my trembling hands and heart.

I took a deep breath, gave him a quick smile and attempted to slow my stride, just a bit, but it was hard. My legs ached with the effort. I was so eager to see dear Nimmie.

Just when I thought I would burst with anticipation, I

saw someone climbing down from the side of the distant wagon, and then there was Nimmie running toward me! Without another thought, I grabbed up my skirts and broke into a headlong run to meet her.

At first neither of us could talk. We just held one another, tears mingling on our faces.

Nimmie was not only my much-missed friend—she held the secrets of the outside world, the world of my family that I loved and missed so much.

By the time we had finished embracing, there was great commotion all around us. Wynn was greeting Nimmie's husband, Mr. McLain, and a crowd of people from the settlement gathered around. The wagon drivers were trying hard to hold the tired teams steady in spite of all of the confusion. Everyone seemed to be talking at once, and Nimmie and I both knew it would be useless to try to visit now. We backed up, looked at one another's face and smiled our delight, our eyes promising each other a long, long talk together as soon as it could be arranged.

But I tried one question: "Katherine?" I queried above the hum.

"She stayed," answered Nimmie. I knew that now was not the time to get more details.

Then the whole party turned toward the settlement, and in almost eerie quietness began to walk the trail that led us over the hills, through the bush, and home.

Nimmie's eyes darted back and forth over the scenery she had not seen for so long. I could sense her straining forward, eager for that first look at the familiar cabins in the small clearing. I knew her thoughts were skipping on ahead of her, but my attention was drawn back to where she had been in the recent past.

I could wait no longer.

"Did you meet my family in Calgary?" I asked, hoping with all of my heart she would be able to say yes.

She turned to me with a light in her eyes.

"They are wonderful!" she exclaimed. "Mary is so sweet;

and the children—I love the children."

I swallowed the big lump suddenly welling up in my throat. How I missed Jon and Mary and their children. I hadn't realized just how much until I heard Nimmie talk about them.

"They are—well?" I struggled with the few words.

"Fine," beamed Nimmie. "But they miss you. They send their love. Little Kathleen begged to come with us so she could see her Aunt Beth. She said it has been 'almost forever' since you left."

My beloved Kathleen—I could almost feel her arms around my neck. The tears sprang again to my eyes.

"I suppose she's grown," I said wistfully.

"Mary says they've all grown a good deal in the past year," responded Nimmie, who of course wouldn't know, having just met the children.

Noticing my tears spilling onto my cheeks, Nimmie quickly changed our conversation.

"They all sent you letters," she told me briskly. "I put them right in the top crate so you could have them just as soon as we get to the settlement. I knew you would be anxious for them."

I reached over to give Nimmie a warm hug. She understood.

The horses seemed to sense rest and food just ahead and hastened their plodding strides. We had to hurry to keep up. Wynn, who had been walking next to Mr. McLain in order to snatch a few pieces of news, joined me, taking my hand to steady my footsteps.

"Are you okay?" he asked after a few silent moments.

I smiled to let him know I was, though I was sure the traces of tears still showed on my face.

"Any news from home?" he asked next.

"Nimmie said they're all fine and they sent letters." My grip on Wynn's hand tightened. "I can hardly wait to read them."

The sun was low on the horizon, making it increasingly

difficult to see the trail. The Indians, with their intimate knowledge of nature and the territory, walked quickly and surely, their steps seeming never to falter. I stumbled now and then and was glad for Wynn's hand. Kip stopped his frisking about and came back to follow closely at my side.

"The McLains will need a place to spend the night, many nights perhaps, until they get themselves settled in the old Lamuir cabin," commented Wynn.

"That's a mess!" I exclaimed, horrified that he would even suggest such a place.

"It can be cleaned up and made quite livable with a little effort," Wynn maintained. "Ian has already asked if it is available." He paused for a moment and then went on slowly, "Like most women, Nimmie might prefer to be on her own."

I knew Wynn was right, at least about Nimmie preferring to be on her own. She was very independent, but oh, it would be nice to keep her with me during the rebuilding of the store.

"I'll help her clean the cabin if that's what she wants," I said rather reluctantly.

"Good," was all Wynn answered.

After we had walked a bit farther, I broke the silence again. "How long do you think it will take to rebuild the trading store?"

"It depends on the weather—how many of the men help, how things go—but Ian says he hopes to have it framed in and ready to shelter the supplies in four weeks or so. Then he will finish the living quarters as time allows."

Poor Nimmie, I groaned inwardly. She would be without a real home for some months, and with the new baby coming that would not be easy.

In the semidarkness I stole another look at Nimmie. She looked fine. She was showing now and I couldn't help but wonder when the baby was due. In my excitement about Nimmie's good news when she had shared her secret, I had not even asked the time of the expected birth. Yes, she could be due before too many weeks passed. Yet she walked with the same straight shoulders, the same confidence, as the rest of her people. I admired Nimmie.

By now it was quite dark. We were still meeting people on their way to welcome the travelers—mothers with little ones in tow, old people who could not hurry with their walking sticks, children who straggled just for the fun of it.

Finally within sight of the small settlement, we could see the dark shapes of the cabins through the gathering night. Hearing the familiar sound of barking dogs as they strained against their unwelcome tethers, I wondered fleetingly if Kip felt a bit smug about the fact that he was with the group, traveling free.

The smoke of the wood fires lingered in the air, though by now most likely every fire in the settlement would have gone out for lack of attention. The sad heap of rubble where the trading post had stood showed faintly through the darkness. I suddenly wished we had taken time to clear it away so that it might not bring returning pain to Nimmie.

I moved closer to her, hoping my presence in the darkness would be some comfort.

It must have been, too, for her voice came softly to me over the creak and grind of the wagons. "It seems like a long-ago bad dream."

Giving her arm a quick squeeze, I did not answer, for I did not know what to say.

We moved silently among the buildings so familiar to both of us as the wagons ground to a stop. The tired drivers lowered their aching bodies to the hard-packed earth, speaking to the teams as they moved forward to tether them until Mr. McLain would give the next orders. Nimmie waited to join her husband, and I spoke to her as I walked by.

"I'll light the fire and get supper ready. As soon as you are free, come to the house. You may wash and rest for a bit before we have our supper."

"Thank you," said Nimmie, her voice soft.

My heart was light as I hurried back home to my supper preparations. Nimmie was back and she looked fine. The much-needed supplies for the village were on the loaded wagons. Soon the trading post would be built again. And after the evening's supper was over and the dishes washed and cared for, Nimmie and I would at last get to have that long-coveted talk.

Chapter Two

Together Again

As I rushed to get the fire started, my mind was busy with what I could fix for our supper. I knew the McLains had been on the trail for many days and would enjoy a full meal rather than a hastily prepared snack. The occasion merited a celebration feast, and yet my pantry was almost bare because of the scarcity of supplies. The wagons that stood in the settlement were loaded down with our future needs, so it wasn't caution that made it impossible for me to fix our guests a really fine meal, even though it was hard to break my habit of conserving during the past weeks. It was simply the fact that there was very little on my shelves to prepare.

I left my fire, the flames now devouring the wood, and began to rummage through the cupboard shelves. It seemed that each container I eagerly pulled forward and opened was almost empty. I wondered just how many more days we could have survived on the little we had left.

There was always meat. The men of the settlement, with Wynn in charge, had kept us well supplied with fresh meat. With the warmer weather, the meat had to be brought to the village daily and divided among the families, as it would not keep fresh for long. I surveyed the piece that had been brought to me for our supper. It had seemed like plenty for Wynn and me, but now, with two others to feed, it looked awfully small.

It was beaver, not my favorite dish, but it was tasty enough. I tried to think of a quick way to cook it—and perhaps stretch it a bit.

I had few vegetables left. But I could make a stew of sorts. I hastened to get it into the pot and on the stove to cook. I had nothing that would make a dessert of any kind. We'd just have to do without, like Wynn and I had been doing.

Thankfully, we had plenty of wood, and the roaring flames soon had the stew simmering in the pot. I wished I had some fresh bread, but we had been rationing our dwindling flour supply. So instead I made some simple biscuits, nearly using up the last of the flour in the tin to do so. I had no shortening on hand except for rendered bear tallow. I did not enjoy the taste of it, but the biscuits would be as hard as rocks without it.

If only I had something special to celebrate this great occasion—the safe return of our friends, the coming of the food supplies. But I had nothing.

And then I remembered the one jar of blueberry preserves I had been hoarding on the top shelf for some special event. *Well, this is a special event!* I enthusiastically went for the blueberries.

Once I had my meal on to cook, the biscuits in the oven, and the table set, there was nothing more for me to do. I fidgeted about, walking the floor from the table to the stove, from the door to the window. I couldn't see anything except shadowy movements in the light from open doors and small, dirt-clouded windows in the distant settlement yard. I knew the wagons were being moved about for unloading. I knew that not all the crates and boxes would be unloaded, for there was no place to store the contents, but a few of the supplies would be organized as quickly as possible so the people of the settlement would have access to them. Tomorrow would be a busy day indeed.

I turned from the window, put more wood in the fire to be sure the pot was kept boiling, and adjusted the dishes and the tableware for the fifth or sixth time. I felt like I was missing out on all the activity in the settlement. Kip must have felt the same way, sensing there was excitement beyond our closed door, for he crossed over to it and stood whining for me to let him out.

I had no sympathy for him. "If I can't go, neither can you," I said firmly. "I'm missing it all, too."

Kip must have known from my voice that I would not let him go, for he whined once more, crossed back to his favorite place in front of the fireplace and lowered himself to the bear rug, looking at me with wide, pleading eyes.

I stirred the stew and pulled the kettle forward for hot water. I had no more tea or coffee. We had used the last of the tea for our Sunday dinner and had been out of coffee for a week or more. We would simply drink the hot water. It really wasn't so bad.

At last I heard footsteps just outside the door, and ran to open it. Nimmie entered the room with her arms full of parcels, chattering as she came in.

"I knew you'd be anxious for your letters, and Mary said I must be sure that you got these parcels right away. The men are bringing the rest."

I felt like Christmas had come with the spring! Dear Mary! I could hardly wait to see what she had sent. I reached for the parcels, prepared to begin tearing off wrappings immediately, and then checked myself. This was not just for me—it was for Wynn also. So instead of ripping away like a child, I squeezed the first parcel a bit, laid it on the nearby chair, and then took the remainder of the parcels from Nimmie and deposited them with the first.

"Wynn said to go ahead and open them," Nimmie encouraged, seeming to read my mind.

"Are you sure?" It wasn't that I doubted her word; it was just that I was so eager I was afraid to trust what I heard.

Nimmie laughed, silvery and soft. I had missed her lovely laugh. There had been so little laughter in the settlement in the past weeks. I hadn't realized just how little until I listened to Nimmie now. Tears misted my eyes. Too much joy was happening too quickly.

I brushed at my eyes with my apron and reached for the first parcel. It was just for me, filled with new yard goods, toilet articles, and some pretty lacey underthings. I ran my hands over each item, feeling its newness and enjoying the fresh scent of something unworn and unwashed.

The next bundle was prepared by the children and contained special sweet treats. There were many things there that children love, but I will admit they looked awfully good to me as well. I couldn't remember when I had eaten something just for the fun of savoring the taste. Each little gift was wrapped and identified. As I read each name, my eyes filled with tears again. There even was a lumpy-looking one from baby Elizabeth, and I knew she had had help. I was sure she had grown in the year I had been gone, but she was still a baby of only two.

The third parcel was from Mary again. It, too, was filled with treats, but of a different sort. There were spices and dried fruits, nuts and teas, vanilla, and a can of *fresh coffee*! Now the tears were really falling. I hadn't tasted some of these things since leaving Calgary. How good they would be! I couldn't express my delight, not even to Nimmie, but I was sure that she understood.

At last I picked up the packet of letters. I would wait to share them with Wynn. I fingered them, turning them over in my hands as I read the names on the envelopes. There was Mary's neat handwriting, the firm script of brother Jon, childish printing from the children and even one in the careless but expressive dash of my sister Julie! I found it hard to wait, but I laid the letters down again.

Getting control of my emotions, I turned to Nimmie. "What would you like to drink with your supper," I asked her, "fresh coffee or an exotic tea?"

Nimmie laughed again. "Well," she answered, "since I have a feeling I might have had fresh coffee and exotic tea since you have, why don't *you* choose?"

I smiled. "I will," I said and took my time deliberating. I debated first over one item and then another, like a child in a candy shop. I was about to select a lemon tea when I thought of Wynn. I was sure, that given a choice, he would pick coffee, so I laid the tea aside and went to open the coffee can. I will never forget that first burst of fragrance—it hung in the air like a promise. I savored it, looking at Nimmie to be sure I wasn't dreaming.

"We need to talk," I said, breathing in the delicious smell of the coffee as I measured it carefully into the pot.

"We will," Nimmie promised. "For as long as you want."

Just then there was a scuffle of feet on the doorstep and Wynn and Ian entered, both men carrying a large crate on their shoulders.

"The family sent rations for the starving Northerners," quipped Wynn, but his tone gave away his heartfelt appreciation for their concern.

"Oh, Wynn!" was all I could say as I looked at the crate.

The men placed it on the floor against the wall. I finally came to my senses enough to offer warm water to Ian so he could wash for supper.

"Sure smells good," Ian boomed out as he sniffed the air. "I get tired awfully fast of campfire cookin'."

"It's not much," I admitted, my cheeks flushing a bit. "I hadn't realized just how low our supplies were until I went to get our supper tonight. I don't know how much further I could have stretched the little bit of food we have left."

"Elizabeth has done a wonderful job of making do," said Wynn, genuine pride in his voice. "She has always found something to go with the meat."

I flushed even more at Wynn's praise. In fact, we both knew that sometimes there had been precious little to go with the meat.

We gathered around our small table, and Wynn led us in prayer. His voice broke a little as he expressed his gratitude to our heavenly Father for getting the wagons to the settlement in time to prevent any real hardship. I was reminded again of the heavy responsibility Wynn had carried over the past months, with the welfare of so many lives on his shoulders.

We did enjoy our simple meal together. Even the beaver meat tasted better with talk and laughter of friends. Nimmie exclaimed over the biscuits. "Bear tallow, isn't it? I've really missed it—tastes so good."

I laughed. I guess one's preferences have a lot to do with one's background.

After the meal the men announced that there were a few more things to be done in the settlement. Wynn lit the lantern and they left, leaving Nimmie and me to clear the table. Without even discussing it, we hurried through the dishes. We were both anxious for that long talk.

At last we settled ourselves. I hadn't yet read our letters, but I still wanted to wait for Wynn. For now I would relish all that Nimmie could tell me about the outside world. In some ways it seemed forever, and yet just yesterday, that I had made the trip by train, barge and wagon over the same trail Nimmie had just traveled.

I really couldn't think where to begin with all my questions. Then I remembered it was Nimmie's first trip "out," away from the settlement. "Well," I said, "what did you think of it all?"

"It was even beyond the books—the feel, the sounds, the big buildings," said Nimmie, her voice filled with excitement, her hands shaping the tall structures as she spoke. "I could not believe that such things really existed. It was all so different—so new."

I looked at Nimmie's shining eyes. I knew she had enjoyed her time out. I wished I could have been with her to show it all to her myself.

"It's wonderful, isn't it?" I spoke softly, remembering so many things, feeling that Nimmie, like me, was already missing the outside world with a hollow ache in her heart.

"Did you hate to come back?" I finally asked, hesitantly.

Nimmie's eyes widened, then softened as she spoke slowly, guardedly, "I loved seeing your world. It truly was fascinating. But as the days and weeks went by, I was so homesick for the rivers, the forests, I could hardly wait to come home."

Chapter Three

Catching Up

When Wynn and Ian returned from the last of the night's duties, Wynn and I read the letters from home while Nimmie and Ian prepared floor-beds for the night.

Our letters confirmed that all of them were well. We were glad to hear that Jon's business was growing, as were his children, and Mary was busy and happy as homemaker. We also learned that after returning home to Toronto, Julie had missed the West so much she had finally persuaded Father and Mother to allow her to return to Calgary in the care of brother Jon. She was now busy giving piano and voice lessons to young Calgary students.

When it came time to retire for the night, Wynn insisted that Nimmie share my bed rather than sleep on the floor, so after we bid our tired husbands good night we went to the bedroom to prepare for bed. We did not go right to sleep but talked until late into the night. There was so much to tell one another, so many questions on my mind. I wanted to hear all about what Nimmie had seen and heard in the outside world. I wanted to know all about my family members, the cities I had left behind, the happenings in the world, the fashions that the ladies were wearing—everything that I had been missing.

Nimmie was more than glad to fill me in, though some

things that she shared with me were seen through different eyes than mine and thus with a different perspective.

I laughed as I listened to Nimmie's frank appraisal of women's fashions. To her the current wearing apparel was very cumbersome and impractical and, for all that matter, not really attractive either—certainly not attractive enough to be worth fussing over.

She had learned to love my family. Though Nimmie did not pretend to totally understand the ways of "the white woman," Mary was kind and generous, and Nimmie could appreciate that characteristic in anyone.

The children in their open, candid way brought much delight to Nimmie. She was especially taken with young Elizabeth. Partly because she bore my name, partly because she was a delightful child, but mostly, admitted Nimmie, because she was still not much more than a baby and Nimmie was looking ahead to the delightful experience of having a child of her own.

I looked at Nimmie. There must have been envy in my eyes, for there certainly was envy in my heart.

"Oh, Nimmie!" I said. "I can hardly wait for your little one." I guess part of what I meant was, *I can hardly wait until it is my turn and I too have a little one, but until then I will gladly share in the joy that your little one brings you.*

Nimmie must have understood my comment for exactly what it was. She looked at me and smiled.

"Soon it will be your turn, Elizabeth. Then our time together will be spent boasting about our babies."

I smiled. I did so much hope that Nimmie was right. I wanted a child so badly.

"Did you see a doctor while you were out?" I asked.

"I really didn't want to—I didn't need to; but Ian was so insistent that I did see one to please him. Everything is just fine."

"I'm glad." I shrugged my shoulder slightly. "And I agree with Ian. I think it's wise that you saw a doctor. Why take chances with the life of your child?"

"I don't see it as 'taking chances,'" stated Nimmie mat-

ter-of-factly. "My people have been having babies without
doctors for many generations."

I wanted to answer, *Yes, and look at the mortality rate,*
but I bit my tongue.

"When is your baby due?" I asked instead.

"Do?" puzzled Nimmie.

"Yes, due?"

"Oh, yes, due," said Nimmie, nodding as she realized my
question. "That means when will it come. Mary asked me
that, too. The doctor said that it would be the fifth day of
August, but I told Ian that nobody tells a baby when to 'due.'
A baby decides that for himself."

Nimmie's comment brought my pillow-smothered laughter. She was right, of course. The baby would decide for himself.

Our chatter turned to other things. Just as I had been
anxious to hear about the outside world, Nimmie was every
bit as interested in catching up on all that had happened in
the settlement in their absence. I brought her up-to-date on
all of our neighbors, though there really didn't seem to be
too much to tell. Our past months had been rather unevent-
ful—and we thanked God for that. We could have had one
tragedy after another, with the food supply so low. God had
kept us, I realized even more as I related to Nimmie how
things had gone in the time since the fire.

At last we agreed that we must get some rest. Tomorrow
would be a busy day with both of us trying to get the small
Lamuir cabin ready for occupancy. Reluctantly we said good
night and let sleep claim us.

The next day, drippy and wet, had ushered in a storm
which seemed to take perverse delight in making everything
miserable for those who had so much to do in the settlement.
The trails were muddy and slippery, and it was difficult just
to walk about, let alone to carry goods or accomplish anything outside.

Nimmie and I made our soggy way to the little cabin. The
one lone window had been broken out, and cracks in the

chinking between the logs let in more than just light. Squirrels had wintered on the one small cupboard shelf, and the floor was covered with wood chips and litter. It was a dismal sight as far as I was concerned, and I was about to say so when Nimmie spoke. "This won't take long!" her tone good-natured and enthusiastic. "We'll have it cleaned up in no time."

I swallowed my protests and picked up the shovel we had brought with us.

My normal cleaning usually began with a pail of hot soapy water. That wasn't possible here in Nimmie's new dwelling. The walls were rough-hewn logs with mud chinking; the floor was hard-packed earth. Scrubbing would have only made mud puddles. Instead, we scraped and shoveled the clutter on the floor and carried it outside by the bucketful, disposing of it behind the cabin. Then Nimmie went to work mixing mud and handfuls of dried grasses. Normally she would have mixed the earth and water first, but the rain had saved her that trouble.

Her hands in mud almost to the elbow, Nimmie got right into the task. I did not envy her; it was hard enough for me to get my hands into bread dough.

When Nimmie was confident she had the right consistency, she began to carefully apply the mud pack to the gaps between the logs. She worked swiftly and skillfully, and I realized as I watched her that she had done such work before. In spite of my fastidiousness, I found myself almost wishing to try my hand at it. Somehow, Nimmie made it look like such a worthwhile skill.

"Would you like me to help?" I finally ventured, half hoping that Nimmie would agree, yet afraid she might.

"It will take me only a few minutes," responded Nimmie. "There is no use for us both to get all dirty."

I went instead to clean the squirrel nest from the shelf.

Nimmie was still working on the logs when I left to prepare a noon meal for us. I sloshed my way through the ever-deepening puddles, hating every squishy step, especially when I slipped and almost fell down.

By the time I reached our cabin my shoes were covered with the heavy gumbo and my skirt hem was soggy and splashed with mud. I surely didn't want to take it all with me into my clean house.

I could think of no way to rid myself of the mess, so reluctantly I opened the door and stepped in. I started with the messy shoes, getting my hands thoroughly mud-covered in the process. Now, how was I going to get out of the dress I was wearing? I should have thought ahead and removed my dress first.

It was too late to think of that. I wiped off my dirty hands near the already muddy hem of my dress, then attempted to lift the dripping mess over my head without dragging the mud over my face and hair. My face streaked with mud, I grumpily left the dress in a sodden heap by the door and headed for the bedroom, my wet feet leaving imprints on the wooden floor.

I felt a little better after I had washed my face and hands, put on a fresh dress and recombed my hair. I found a dry pair of shoes and went back to my kitchen to build the fire and prepare our meal.

I was glad for the heat of the fire. I hadn't noticed it till then, but the cold rain and the early spring day was chilly— and so was I. Nimmie probably would be cold when she arrived as well. And the menfolk, working out in the rain all morning, would be chilled to the bone. We would be fortunate if no one caught a dreadful cold from the ordeal. I decided to have some hot soup ready for lunch.

The men were busy now preparing to uncrate and distribute much-needed supplies which had arrived with the McLains. If only there was a building big enough to hold all of it out of the rain.

Instead, everyone would be forced to puddle through the mud around the wagons.

I had the meal ready and the room warm when Nimmie came for dinner. She was wet to the skin but did not complain. She had no other clothes unpacked so I loaned her some of mine. She was not quite as careful as I had been about leaving all her mess at the door, but then, I reminded myself, Nimmie had spent many years living in houses that didn't even have floors.

The menfolk soon joined us. They too were sopping wet but they shrugged off the need for warm, dry clothes. "We'll be just as wet in a few minutes anyway," Wynn insisted.

Wynn knew my concern for my clean house so he announced that they would take their dinner by the door. I tried to argue with him but he was adamant. Nimmie quietly took the two chairs and placed them by the door as Wynn requested, and, seeing that I was the loser on this one, I went ahead and served up their bowls of steaming soup.

In a short while they were stepping out the door into the chilling rain again. I worried, sure that pneumonia was in store for both of them.

Wynn was soon back. He stood at the open door and called to me so he wouldn't need to bring more mud into the cabin.

"Elizabeth," he said when I joined him at the door, "I hate to ask this, but I have no choice. We are going to need to bring the supply crates in here so that we can sort them out without the rain ruining the foodstuff. It's the only place in the whole settlement that is anywhere near big enough to work."

I'm sure he saw the momentary horror on my face, but I quickly recovered and nodded my head.

"You understand?" asked Wynn and I could detect the hesitancy in his voice.

"Of course," I managed to answer. "That will be fine— just fine."

Wynn looked searchingly at me, nodded his thanks, then turned to go.

"We'll be back as soon as we can hitch the horses to the wagons."

I allowed myself a big sigh and went back to join Nimmie for our dinner. I would need to hurry to clean up the dinner dishes. Soon our cozy little nest would be a shambles.

Chapter Four

Supply House

Even though I had tried to brace myself for the intrusion into my home, I found I was totally unprepared for what happened.

The rain of course did not help matters. Everyone who came through the door brought with him mud and water that gathered on my wooden floor in dirty little puddles—which eventually got to be big puddles.

There was no use trying to clean them up. The men came in a steady stream, groaning under the weight of the crates and boxes. At first all of the supplies were stored in Wynn's office room, but soon that was filled to overflowing and the men began to stack the boxes in our living area.

I knew as well as anyone that the need for those supplies was now. I knew too that there simply was no other place in the village where they could be unpacked. It was unthinkable to try to sort and distribute it all in the rain.

By the time the last of the boxes were stacked high in our small quarters, our house no longer looked like a home. Nimmie, who had been the traffic director, of sorts, found one of their boxes, and with hammer in hand, busied herself looking for dry clothes for Ian. This reminded me that, with the boxes now all inside, Wynn, too, would be able to change into dry clothes. As Wynn shut the door for the last time and the

men with the teams climbed aboard to drive off, leaving deep
ruts in what had been our front path, I turned to Wynn and
implored him to take the time to change his wet clothes.

He did not argue but went to the bedroom, unbuttoning
his shirt as he went, not wanting to waste time. I mournfully
watched the muddy tracks as they followed him out of the
room.

Without comment to our two guests, I went for the mop
pail and the mop.

As soon as Wynn had returned from the bedroom, looking
much better and safer in dry clothes, Nimmie sent Ian in to
change from his wet things.

Wynn reached for the mop. "Here, let me, Elizabeth," he
offered, but I held on to it.

"You have enough to do without mopping floors," I told
him. "I can't do much, but I can at least do this."

Wynn looked at the heaped-up crates and nodded his head.
Ian soon joined him and the two went to work. With hammers
pounding and boards squeaking their protest, the sacks, tins
and cartons with their intriguing labels—flour, tea, coffee,
sugar, and such—began to stack all around us.

I looked at Nimmie, hoping she would suggest we head
for her temporary cabin again, but she didn't. Instead, she
began sorting things into piles. I gathered my energy up and
joined her.

We worked for hours, and then I looked at the clock and
checked with Wynn.

"Would you like me to fix us a cup of tea?"

He straightened rather slowly, placing a hand on the small
of his back, and he too looked at the clock—seven minutes
to four. We had been working without a break since our noon
meal.

"That would be nice, Elizabeth," he answered. "We could
use that."

I went to work on it right away. I wished I had something
special to go with the tea. But the cold biscuits from the night
before spread with some jam Mary had sent would help to

refresh us some. Our dinner soup did not stick to the ribs for long when we were working so hard.

The men did not sit and sip their tea. I feared they might burn their mouths, but they were soon back at their task.

It was shortly after five when Ian went to the door and began hammering on a tin drum. *What a strange way to celebrate the unpacking of the last crate of the day,* I thought.

Ian saw my questioning look and smiled a tired smile. "It's the dinner bell," he told me.

"The dinner bell?" My eyes traveled again to the clock.

"We told them that we'd call them when we got the supplies unpacked so they could come and get something to prepare for their suppers."

"Oh!" I nodded in understanding. Many of the Indian people probably had nothing in their homes with which to prepare a meal, except perhaps a little meat from the day before. No hunting detail would have been assigned on this day as every available back had been bent to the task of getting the crates unloaded.

As soon as Ian's call rang out, lines of hungry people began to form at our door and make their way through to hold out baskets, pails or pots to be filled with food for their evening meal.

It seemed like the rain-soaked stream would never stop— and stream it truly was. My mopped-up floor was soon a river of muddy water again.

Wynn stopped doling out supplies long enough to ask me to start a fire in the fireplace. Our door was constantly open and the room was chilly with the damp air.

Seeing the relief and gratitude in the hungry eyes of those who came, I quickly chose to ignore the muddy water that ran from their clothes and feet and thanked the Lord instead that the supplies had arrived in time. I marveled that we had actually managed to make it through the tough months of early spring without disease and death overtaking the village.

I smiled at the hollow faces and the outstretched hands,

often saying a few words in their native language to welcome them to my home and to express my thankfulness that they and their families had stayed well.

It was dark now and the evening air was close to freezing. The rain clouds would keep actual frost away, but the line of people at our door—mostly women, with an occasional girl or a man holding out the container—certainly would have a cold walk home.

No one lingered. They were concerned with one thing only—to get their needs for the evening meal and to hurry home to their fires so they might prepare it for the family.

My own household needed an evening meal too. I did not as yet have my own food supplies replenished. Our boxes had been stacked in a pile at the far end of the room. There was not room for me to open them in the already crowded room, so I gave up the idea of heading for the corner with hammer in hand. The leftovers from the big pot of stew I had made the night before would have to do.

I got out the cold stew and put it on to heat. Then I set to work making another batch of bear-tallow biscuits. I nearly choked at the thought of eating them for yet another meal. I had so looked forward to having something new from the supplies—so near yet so out of reach!

The men would not stop to eat until every home in the settlement had been supplied. It was late by then. Nimmie and I had already nibbled on the biscuits. With hunger gnawing at me, I had to admit they tasted rather good. Especially when I spread them with Mary's jam.

It was almost eight o'clock when the door finally closed and the tired men straightened up and reached for a chair. I dished up our overheated stew, put out the now-cold biscuits and we gathered around the table.

Our table prayer was a little longer that night. In a reverent voice, Wynn expressed his thanks to God that the people of the village would not go to bed hungry on this night. I knew he felt it very deeply.

There was no room left on the floor for the McLains to

spread their fur robes. Wynn suggested that he and Ian take the furs and blankets and go to the Lamuir cabin, and Nimmie stay with me again.

I wanted to protest. Not that I wasn't glad to share my bed with Nimmie, but I didn't like to think of Wynn, as tired as he was, sleeping on the floor in a cold cabin. The window still was not fixed. That was Ian's job as soon as he discovered where the glass had been packed. There was no wood for a fire. The mud walls were not thoroughly dry in the damp, rainy atmosphere. It would not be a nice place to spend the night.

Nimmie protested, answering us that she was quite able to sleep in the cabin, but Wynn insisted that she stay in our house; and Ian, rather reluctantly, supported him.

In ordinary circumstances, Nimmie could have slept on our cot, but even that was stacked high with sorted-out supplies.

At last the men ventured back out in the damp night, their arms filled with blankets and furs which had been bundled in slickers to protect them from the rain.

Nimmie and I were too tired to spend any more time talking. We simply stacked up dirty supper dishes and headed for the bed. I did not even stop to wash all that mud from my floor.

Chapter Five

A New Day

A soft stirring in the cabin aroused me from a deep sleep. With my wakefulness also returned a consciousness of my circumstances. It was Nimmie who shared my bed, not Wynn.

Nimmie needed all the rest the all-too-short night would afford her, I thought as I slipped cautiously out from the covers and dressed in the semidarkness. The men would soon be looking for their breakfast. I tiptoed from the room, shoes in hand, and carefully closed the door behind me.

In the soft light of the oil lamp I found Wynn back at work on the supplies. I could tell by the way he moved that he was making great effort to be quiet—which of course hampered his agility. He looked up when he heard me.

"Did I waken you? I'm sorry. I tried—"

"That's fine. I needed to be up anyway. I have so much to do and—"

My eyes traveled to the table where I had left dirty dishes the night before. They were all gone. I looked then at the floor I was dreading to clean. The mud too was gone. I glanced back at Wynn, embarrassed that he should have needed to do housework in addition to his other tasks. He was reaching for a hammer. With the loud bang, I let out a little gasp. The hammer stopped mid-swing and Wynn's eyes met mine.

"What's wrong?" he asked, the hammer still poised for the strike.

"You'll waken Nimmie and she needs—"

"Nimmie?" Wynn said cheerfully. "Nimmie was up and left for her cabin the minute I arrived, and that was almost an hour ago."

He turned his attention to his task.

I blinked. How had Nimmie wakened, dressed and left the room without me hearing her?

Wynn finished with the board and laid aside the hammer.

"I invited them for breakfast again. After that they expect to be on their own."

"So soon? Their window isn't even fixed."

"Ian's working on it right now, and Nimmie is busy doing the rest of the cleaning. They expect to move all their things out of here this morning. Then Nimmie says we should be able to have our living room back again—at least most of it."

"I'm sorry about the dishes and the floor—" I began, but Wynn stopped me in puzzlement.

"Sorry about what?"

"That you had to clean up."

"I didn't clean up."

"You didn't?"

"It looked just like this when I got here."

"Nimmie!" I said, the light finally beginning to dawn. "Nimmie must have gotten up and cleaned everything early this morning."

Wynn nodded in agreement, his attention back on what he was doing.

"And I was sleeping," I chided myself.

"I've found you some supplies," Wynn remarked, seeming not to have heard the scolding I was giving myself.

Supplies? Our supplies! I hurried over to Wynn and peered into the box he was opening.

"This is just flour, sugar, salt and such," said Wynn. "You might be more interested in those other two boxes. They came from Mary and Jon.

It seems forever since I have seen so many good things. I rejoiced as I stacked the treasures around me. Mary and Jon had thought of everything. They had even packed fresh fruit and vegetables. The Calgary newspaper piled up on the floor as I unwrapped item after item. There were even fresh eggs and butter.

I was about to crumple the newspaper out of the way. "Save that, would you please," Wynn suggested. "We'll even get to catch up on some world news, thanks to Mary's foresight." Carefully I began to smooth out each sheet of newspaper, sorry that in my eagerness I had unwrapped so hastily and carelessly.

When I turned to the kitchen, eager to get at the special breakfast I was planning with all my wonderful new supplies, Wynn was carrying armloads to our storeroom and arranging the things for our future use. Already a welcome little square of our floor was beginning to show. How I looked forward to having my house neat and orderly again.

By the time I had our sumptuous breakfast of fried eggs, jam, fresh oranges, bran muffins and oatmeal porridge ready, I heard Nimmie's and Ian's voices as they came up the path. Peering out the window, I noted it was still raining. *This day will be no more pleasant than yesterday,* I groaned.

Wynn opened the door for our guests, and I began to dish up the food for the table. On the back of my stove stood a bubbling pot of potatoes. I just couldn't wait to taste some. We had been without potatoes for weeks! I had told myself as I peeled them before breakfast that I would cook them to fry up for our noon meal. Now as I sniffed their fragrance, I knew I had been fooling myself—I'd never wait for dinner. A bit shamefaced, I put them in a dish and set them on our breakfast table.

After everyone was seated and the morning prayer said, I reached first for the bowl containing the potatoes. Yes, the oatmeal would surely taste good, the oranges would be a wonderful treat. And I could hardly wait for a bran muffin with real butter rather than dry biscuits. But the thing I wanted most was a good helping of potatoes, even if it was breakfast.

"This is silly, I know," I said, blushing, "but I just can't wait for a taste of potatoes again. I never realized how much I missed them until I saw them there this morning, all fresh and round, without wrinkles in their skins or sprouts all over them."

Ian smiled and winked at Nimmie in understanding. I sprinkled salt and pepper, dabbed on some real butter and lifted a forkful of potatoes to my mouth. They were just as good as I had expected them to be. I savored the mouthful, enjoying it to the full.

Wynn, too, bypassed the oatmeal and reached for the steaming bowl. "You're going to have potatoes, too?" I asked, surprised.

"Sure am," he laughed. "I was afraid when I smelled them cooking that you were going to make me wait for our noon meal. I was wondering how I might sneak a few from the pot without getting caught."

We all had a good laugh. Nimmie and Ian allowed us our potatoes, and they ate the oatmeal and muffins.

After breakfast Ian went for the team and wagon so their things could be taken to the cabin in a single trip. The rain had slackened, but their belongings still needed to be tucked under canvas.

With the removal of all that belonged to the McLains, and our things being put in the storage room, Wynn had more room to organize the rest of the supplies. Little by little he was getting it cleared away to the room he called his office.

I did my best to help him. He would not let me lift the heavier things, and I had to ask about most of the items I did move, to be sure that I stacked them where he would be able to find them.

By midday we had some paths through our living area, and the cot was discovered and unloaded. Kip was even able to get back to his favorite place before the fire.

I went back to the kitchen to prepare our meal, again
cooking potatoes. I also cooked carrots and parsnips and tur-
nips. It was a strange combination, but they all looked so
good to me. I made up some cole slaw and informed Wynn
that our dinner was ready. It wasn't until we sat down that
I realized I hadn't prepared any meat. I was really tired of
meat, but I wondered if Wynn would miss it. If he did he
didn't mention it. Instead, he talked about how good the vegetables were.

In the afternoon Wynn finished stacking the supplies for
the villagers. Almost every inch of his office floor was covered, and the stacks reached almost to the ceiling.

Then Wynn went to work at the one little window in the
room. Curious, I watched to see what he was doing. He was
making a shelf that extended both inside and outside at the
bottom edge of the window. He didn't wait for me to ask what
it was for.

"I'm making a shelf so I can distribute the supplies from
here and then people won't need to enter the house to get
them."

I pictured a long line of hungry, cold, damp people, standing in queue for their daily rations.

"But they can't wait out there in the rain," I protested,
willing to forego the clean floors for their comfort.

"They have to wait in the rain anyway," Wynn explained.
"They can't all fit in our living room at once."

Realizing he was right, I returned to my kitchen and took
a few moments to pray that the rain would stop.

Ian came back, a large ledger in his hand. The Indians
had been told to wait for the sound of the crude gong before
lining up for more supplies. Those of the previous night had
been given out at no charge, with deep thankfulness that
God had seen us through. Now the books would need to be
kept. Each man in the village had his winter's catch of furs,
and the tally would be kept on account until the day that
McLain could take in the furs to settle the accounts. First he
would need to construct his new trading post.

As soon as Ian pounded on the drum with the hammer, the line began to form. Though it had not stopped raining, it had slowed down considerably. I thanked God for that.

Today there was happy chatter among the women who stood in the line. They could finally believe that the supplies were really here, enough for each day's need rather than just a fleeting dream of relief.

As Wynn distributed supplies to them, one by one, Mr. McLain busily entered the items to each one's account. Now the women were given a choice of purchase. Yesterday they all had been allotted the same items to prepare a meal.

It was getting dark before the last of the line was waited on. Wynn closed the window and turned to Ian.

"Is this going to work?" he asked him.

"Perfect," exulted Ian. "I'm glad you thought of the shelf. Nimmie will be settled by tomorrow, and she will be able to take your place. We know you can't spend all of your time dishing out store supplies."

"I'm glad to help until you are settled a bit, but I do need to get back on the trail again. There are a number of people I should check on as quickly as possible."

"We understand," Ian assured him. "Nimmie and I should be quite able to handle this from now on."

"But how about the building of the new store?" asked Wynn.

Ian pondered. It was true. He was going to be more than busy. His building skills and direction were needed on the project. Even though there were a number of men who would be happy to work for Ian, they could not proceed without supervision. Ian would need to be available every part of every day.

"We'll have to work out something," Ian was saying when I broke in hesitantly from the doorway. "I'll help Nimmie if you'll just show me what you want done."

Both of the men swung to look at me.

Wynn broke the silence. "There you are," he said to Ian with a grin.

Mr. McLain looked relieved. "You mean that?" he asked me.

"Of course. I'd be glad to."

"How about keeping the ledger?"

"The ledger?"

"Recording what is given to each family. Nimmie will tell you what to write."

"That would be fine," I stammered out. "I'm sure—sure I could handle that."

"I'm sure you could, too," said McLain confidently. "Then Nimmie could work with the people. It would be a bit easier for her, some of the people not knowing much English and you not understanding much of their language yet."

I liked his reasoning. Nimmie could wait on the customers and I could work along with her and keep the accounts. I was going to have her around after all!

In the meantime I hoped that the building project would go quickly. I was thankful for the supplies for the people. I would also be thankful to reclaim my home. I looked around at the stacked-up supplies. Our house looked so much better than it had just that morning, though Wynn's small office was not free for his use, and many things were still piled along the walls in our living quarters. Yes, I hoped with all of my heart that the building of the new trading post would go well.

Chapter Six

Routine

Early the next morning the clouds began to break up and the heavy rain that had fallen during the night gradually diminished to a drizzle. I began to be hopeful that the rain might actually stop.

By midafternoon the sun was actually peeping out from among the clouds now and then. I got out my washtub so I could launder the wet, dirty clothes of the preceding days and get them on the line.

I worked quickly, for I knew there wasn't much time until Nimmie would arrive and clang the drum for the evening supply line.

I had just hung the last item on the line, thrown out my wash water and returned to my kitchen when I glanced out the window to see Nimmie coming up the path, dry and in her own clothing for the first time since she had returned to the settlement. Her feet were not free of the cumbersome mud, however. She looked like she was wearing brown snowshoes as she plodded along, carefully lifting one mud-packed foot after the other as she made her way up to our door.

I called for her to come in as I pushed the kettle forward onto the heat for a cup of tea before beginning our store duties. She didn't enter but called back to me from the doorway, "Could you bring me some water, please, so that I might wash my feet?"

I poured warm water into the basin, threw a towel over my arm and went to the door.

Nimmie had not bothered to wear anything on her feet. Knowing that the mud would cake as she walked, she came barefoot. It was much easier to clean feet than to clean shoes. She sat on the step and washed her feet in the basin. She refused the clean towel. "They're not clean enough for that," she protested. "Just give me an old rag." She dried her feet on a rag I found, swished out the basin and came in, shutting the door behind her.

"Isn't it great to see the sun again?" she exclaimed as she settled in a chair. I agreed as I poured our tea.

When we had emptied our teacups, we went to the storage room. Nimmie showed me how to record the items under each family's name in the ledger and then went out to call the villagers while I opened the window for our first customers.

At first it was novel and rather fun, but by the time we had measured and served, recorded and changed, argued and pleased each of our customers, I think both of us were ready to call it a day.

Wynn had gone to make some of his calls. He had no idea when he would be back so could not give me a time for the evening meal. I would have it ready and try to keep it as warm and palatable as possible, hoping that he wouldn't be too late.

Nimmie left in the semi-dusk to prepare a meal for Ian. He along with several other men had left for the woods that morning to mark out trees for felling. Nimmie did not know the hour for her evening meal either.

One thing we did know: We were both glad that it was no longer raining.

The days that followed were much like that first one. I hurried through my housework so I could accomplish what needed to be done for the day. I am sure that Nimmie did the same.

Each day the paths became a little drier, so the rutted pathway up to our door was no longer slippery with mud. I even tried to smooth out the ruts in the path, much to Nimmie's amusement.

The settlement teemed with new life and busyness. The women searched through the woods for edible spring growth for the cooking pots. Some of the men, under Ian's direction, felled trees while others cleared away the debris left from the fire at the old trading post. Stakes in the ground marked where the new post would stand, a bit larger than the first one. The living quarters at the back would be for Nimmie and Ian and the children they were anxiously looking forward to having. There would be no living quarters needed for Katherine. She had decided to go back to teaching in the Edmonton area.

Each day Wynn again took to the trail. Because the paths were free of the winter's snow, the dog team was not usable now, so Wynn's trips were even harder than normal. Swollen rivers and streams made journeys by canoes risky. With the return of the sun, the mosquitoes hatched in great numbers. The trail was not a pleasant place to be, but it was part of his job; and so without complaint, Wynn shouldered the pack with his emergency supplies and his noon lunch and left each morning at sunrise.

Nimmie and I soon established a daily routine. She would arrive promptly at three, we would have an afternoon cup of tea or coffee, and then we would bang on the drum and signal the ladies that the settlement "store" was open for business.

The sun shone on some days, the rain fell on others. Gradually a framework was taking shape in the settlement as the men worked under Ian's direction. Wynn helped when his duties did not call him elsewhere.

Wynn had found a few trappers who really had needed help, men who lived alone and did not come into the village after the winter's trapping was over. One man had been sick for over two weeks; he finally had become so weak he was unable to care for himself. Wynn traveled out to his cabin every other day to prepare food and give him medicine. Another man also had been sick, but by the time Wynn found him he was too far gone to recover. Though Wynn nursed him for several days, giving him the medicine he had available, he sorrowfully turned from being doctor to undertaker and parson, finally committing the man to the earth he had been so close to for so many years.

The mosquitoes and blackflies swooped around in droves. It was hard to remember they had been just as miserable the year before. I had to get used to them all over again.

Nimmie and I planted our gardens with seeds she had brought back. I could hardly wait for them to sprout and the tender plants to make their appearance. Nimmie was far more patient than I.

Nimmie's delivery time was drawing nearer. She didn't seem to feel anything other than anticipation, but for some reason, I felt alarm.

What if something goes wrong? What will we do if we need a doctor? For the first time I began to feel just a little thankful that I wasn't the one waiting for the arrival of a baby. I had not shared my prayers with Wynn, but for some weeks I had been praying nightly that God would see fit to grant my desire for a family—and soon. We had already been married for almost a year and it seemed like God should be answering my prayer by now.

Still, as I looked at Nimmie, daily becoming larger and heavier, I felt the shiver of fear run through me. *Perhaps it would be easier if I were facing the birth myself*, I thought, *instead of knowing that my dear friend is the one who will be going through the birth pains.* At any rate, I found myself thinking more and more about Nimmie's impending delivery time. I prayed more earnestly for her and the baby than I had ever prayed for anything in my entire life.

"Please, dear God," I pleaded daily, almost hourly, "please let everything be all right."

Chapter Seven

Life Goes On

By now the new trading post was far enough along for the supplies to be taken over and arranged inside the empty shell. Mr. McLain knew that Wynn needed his one-room office and that I was anxious to have my living quarters back.

The men again tracked through my house to load the wagons with everything that belonged to the store owner. I was relieved to see it go, and yet a little sadness tugged at me too. I had enjoyed the feeling of being needed in the little settlement.

I felt better when we decided that Nimmie and I would continue the distribution; instead of Nimmie coming to my house, now I would make the daily trek into the village.

I had not been there much in the past weeks, simply having no reason to go. Nimmie had come to my house daily, and I saw almost every woman of the village on a regular basis when they came for supplies. And our supplies for the next several months were stored in our own storage room.

Though I had not really missed the little excursions into the village, Kip had. He was restless. I tried to take him for a walk each morning as soon as I had finished my household chores, but he continued to whine at the door.

I had no time to romp with him like I used to and I was afraid to let him out on his own. I was sure he would head for the village and the other dogs, and even though he was no longer a pup, I still did not relish the prospect of a fight. I was sure one would occur if Kip were allowed to run free. I was especially determined to keep him away from Buck, the village fighter, for just as long as possible—my preference was "forever." But at least I wanted to be sure Kip was full grown so he might have some chance of holding his own. Buck was an experienced fighter and he was mean. No way did I want Kip tangling with him.

So I ran down wooded paths and trails by the river whenever I could work it into my morning schedule, just to make sure Kip's muscles got some exercise, and in the afternoons when Nimmie and I were busy as storekeepers, I kept him in.

Then even those runs were cut back.

Nimmie and I had been missing our Bible studies together, so we decided that even though we were busy, we would try to work one in each week on Wednesdays. That meant our other duties had to be crowded into the rest of the mornings of the week.

Both the gardens were doing well. We were proud and excited about the growing vegetables. I could hardly wait until they would be big enough to serve. But the garden, too, took work. Though plants grew quickly in the summer sun, the weeds seemed to do even better. It was a big job to keep up with them.

So the summer was a busy one, each day bringing us closer to the first of August. From then on, I wondered if I would be able to sleep for thinking of Nimmie and the coming baby.

One afternoon as I left the house to go to the settlement for the afternoon store hours, my thoughts were busy with Nimmie and the little one she was expecting. When I moved to the door, Kip was there by my side, pushing against me to get out, his eyes pleading as he looked at me and whined. It had been several days since his last run.

He looked so pitiful, his big blue eyes turned to mine.

"All right," I said, "you can come. But you've got to be good. You'll have to lie quietly in the corner while I do my work."

Kip's tail began to wag as he recognized the consent in my voice.

We walked the short distance to the settlement together, Kip managing to get in quite a few side trips. When we reached the store, Kip obediently lay down in the corner I pointed out to him and stayed there.

With the noise of the hammers and hand saws all around us, Nimmie and I often had to raise our voices to one another to get our instructions understood.

The customers did not need to come as often now. The women had organized their households to the point where they had the basics, and many of them were now taking daily trips to the woods for fresh foods. I'm sure they welcomed the additions to their diets as joyfully as I had done.

Nimmie urged me to leave a little early, saying she would stay for a while in case any others came. I called Kip to heel and we started out for our cabin.

I was not paying much attention to Kip as we walked toward home through the late afternoon sunshine. My thoughts were again with Nimmie. She hadn't said anything, but I thought I noticed weariness about her eyes and slower movements than usual. Was I only imagining it?

As I walked through the settlement, the dogs barked and growled at me, straining at their leashes. I'm sure what provoked them most was seeing Kip invading their territory. I still respected their turf and made sure I detoured a good distance from their tethered ground, but I did not have the fear I once had.

Since there was now plenty of food for the village dogs, they had become round and fluffy again rather than looking mangy and shaggy as they had through the difficult winter months. I decided there was really no reason for their being so aggressive and nasty, so I paid little attention to them. In choosing to ignore the dogs, I tried not to antagonize them.

There was no love lost between them and me as they bared their fangs and growled whenever they felt Kip and me getting too close.

Kip ran along beside me, heeling whenever I commanded. We were as yet not far enough out of the village to allow him his side trips. He was still the prettiest dog in the settlement. Wynn said he was now his full height, though he might still put on a few pounds. He was soft and fluffy with the beautiful silver tip to his fur. The children loved him, and even those who had been viciously bitten by a village dog in the past had learned that it was safe to reach out a hand to Kip. Many of the children would wrap their arms around his neck or have a friendly tussle with him on the floor of our cabin.

We were just reaching the last village cabin and I was about to let Kip run free when I saw the hackles raise on his neck. It was not often that Kip responded in this way and I hesitated, wondering what was wrong. My first thought was that some small wild animal had strayed into the village— perhaps a nasty smelling skunk.

And then I saw *him*. Rushing toward us was Buck, lips curled back and teeth exposed. His hackles were up, too, and I knew that this time Kip would take the challenge. With a flash I remembered the long-ago day when Buck had rushed at Kip, then hardly more than an overgrown pup. He had backed off that time in submission to the older dog. But Kip's pose was not one of submission now. He was a full-grown dog, and he had his pride.

Buck stopped a few feet short of Kip. I called Kip to heel again, but he acted like he had never heard my voice before nor learned what the word meant. He stepped sideways as though to feel out his ground and make sure of his footing.

I watched in fascinated horror as Buck came in closer and Kip did not back away. His own teeth bared in a snarl and I heard a rumble from deep in his throat.

Slowly they began to circle one another, eyes blazing, throats voicing challenges and threats; and then there was a sudden lunge forward. I don't know which dog made the

first move. I only know they met in midair and shrieked out
their rage as bodies clashed and teeth tore.

Both dogs had the protection of a heavy coat. Knowing
that, they aimed for throat, for eyes, for face, each time they
came together. They struck with lightning fury and then
tumbled in the dust of the path, rolling over and over, with
grunts and snarls and sharp yips of rage or pain.

I stood rooted to the spot, wanting to stop them, wanting
to run, wanting to scream for someone to do *something*! But
I did nothing, only lifted my hands to my face and prayed
that it would soon be over.

Horrified, I was too dumbstruck to even cry. Would it
never end? They would break and circle and then rush at one
another again, falling this way and that, striking for each
other's face or a leg in an effort to fell the opponent. I could
see that Kip was bleeding. He had a gash on his cheek that
was spilling blood as he rolled back and forth in the dirt.

But Kip wasn't the only one with an injury. Buck, too,
was bleeding on his neck from a torn, ragged cut. Still they
lashed and rolled. Over and over, their heads whipping this
way and that to strike at their opponent and then jerk clear
of his counter strike. *This is terrible!* I moaned.

At last, with one quick move, Kip clasped Buck's leg in
his teeth and crunched down hard. The older dog screamed
in pain and flipped himself forward to jerk free. Kip held
firm and as Buck hurled himself away, I heard a sickening
snap.

Again they struck, but it was clear that Buck's front right
leg was held up and that it had been broken.

I found my voice then. I screamed for them to stop. As
much as I feared and disliked Buck, I did not want to see
him injured further. Nor did I want to take chances on Kip
getting hurt any more. In spite of his injury, Buck still was
determined to lick the younger dog. With a ferociousness I
had never seen before, he struck again and another tear appeared on the side of Kip's jaw.

"Stop it!" I screamed. "Stop it, both of you! Stop it, do you hear?" But I was totally ignored.

They pulled away and circled again, Buck skillfully trying to maneuver on his three good legs. They were both panting heavily, their tongues lolling and their sides heaving.

"Stop it!" I yelled again. "Stop it! Go home, Buck. Go home. Kip, heel." But they paid no heed to my words.

It was Kip who jumped first. He aimed another blow at Buck's already torn and bleeding ear, and the big husky yelped in pain and rage.

And then it was over, as quickly as it had begun. Buck was gone, his tail tucked submissively between his legs, his one leg held aloft as he ran.

I ran to Kip and fell to my knees beside him.

"Bad dog," I scolded him, tears streaming down my face. "Bad dog. You shouldn't fight. Don't you know that you shouldn't fight? It's bad to fight. It's bad to fight unless you really have to." And suddenly I realized that Kip really had to. Buck had challenged him.

"Come on," I said, "I'll take you home."

I led him to the cabin. He heeled beautifully, just as he had been taught. I walked quickly, wanting to get him to the safety of his rug before the fireplace, where I could check and tend his wounds.

After I had closed the door securely behind us, I knelt beside him again and ran my fingers over his body. He was still trembling. His face was blood-covered from the two ragged gashes on his cheeks, but other than that he seemed to be fine.

I started to cry again as I held him. He must have wondered what was wrong with me. I trembled every bit as much as he did.

"You licked him, you crazy dog," I told him. "You licked the big bully. I didn't want you to, but you did. You licked the meanest dog in the whole village."

I straightened up and wiped my tear-streaked face. My voice became firm. "Now you won't have to fight again—ever. Do you hear?"

Chapter Eight

Surprises

A kiss on the nose awoke me. I struggled to open my eyes and focus them properly. Wynn was leaning over me. He reached out and brushed back some wayward hair from my face.

"Do you know what day it is, Elizabeth?" he asked me.

It seemed like rather a foolish question to me, but I struggled to make my brain work so that I might come up with the proper answer.

"It's Friday," I said, puzzled that he had asked.

He chuckled softly and kissed me again.

"It's more than Friday, my dear. It's our first anniversary."

I jerked upright, nearly catching Wynn's chin with my head.

"Really?"

Wynn avoided my charge. "Really!" he said, laughing at me again.

Anniversaries were supposed to be special occasions— maybe a night out, dinner and candlelight. There would be no such thing here in Wynn's northland. I didn't think I could even find a candle. Candles were not necessary when only oil lamps were burned.

"Oh, Wynn," I moaned, "I forgot all about it. I don't have anything special planned."

"I do," said Wynn. "At least I hope you'll think it special. Remember that camping trip you've been begging for? The one where we will sleep out under the stars?"

I nodded, my eyes wide in anticipation.

"Well, how would you like to take that trip today?"

I squealed and threw my arms around Wynn's neck. I guess he took that for my answer.

"I have everything packed and ready to go," he said. "We can leave just as soon as we have our breakfast."

It didn't take me long to get out of bed, dressed and have breakfast on the table.

Kip sensed the excitement and whined at the door, fearful that we might go without him. I patted his head and assured him he could go.

As soon as I had cleared away the breakfast things, I gathered a few personal items I wanted to take and placed them with the packs Wynn had made. I knew Wynn was far more knowledgeable than I about what was needed on an overnight campout, but I still couldn't stop myself from asking, "Did you remember the matches? Are you sure you have all the food we'll need?"

Wynn just laughed at me and told me to trust him.

We were finally packed up and on our way, Kip frisking on ahead. Each with a backpack—Wynn's quite a bit heavier than mine—we walked for most of the morning and came to the most beautiful spot beside a small pond made by beavers damming the stream. The fir trees, thick about us, made a canopy over our heads. It looked just perfect.

"Here is where we stop," said Wynn, much to my delight.

Wynn insisted on setting up camp, and I just wandered about, taking in all of the beauty around me. Wynn cut spruce boughs for our mattress and then spread our furs and blankets to make a soft bed. It looked so inviting when he was finished that I knew I wouldn't miss our bed at home.

Wynn even fixed our meal, saying that this anniversary

was my day off. I laughed and let him humor me.

We washed the dishes together in the little stream nearby and then sat with our backs against a fallen log while we watched the beavers work.

It was our first opportunity to really talk for weeks, so with our fingers intertwined, we talked softly while we watched the beaver couple. We spoke of many things, some little and foolish, others more important and part of our inner dreams and plans for the future.

I learned much about my husband on that camping trip. I had thought I already knew him well, but he shared with me so many new things—about his childhood, about his training, about his desires and goals.

I shared my thoughts and feelings with Wynn, too. I think he guessed part of my desires when I spoke about Nimmie and her coming baby with such wistfulness.

"You'd like a child, wouldn't you, Elizabeth?" more a statement than a question.

"Oh, so much," I told him. "I can hardly wait. And here we have been married for a whole year and . . ." I did not finish the sentence for fear Wynn would somehow think I was blaming him. "God knows when the time is right," I finished instead.

Wynn nodded and we talked of other things.

Wynn took me for walks and showed me flora and fauna I would never have spotted.

Our evening meal was not by candlelight, nor was it a gourmet feast at a fancy restaurant. But I wouldn't have traded it for anything in the world.

Wynn fixed it over an open fire, roasting freshly caught fish slowly until done to perfection and serving them with vegetables he had brought from our garden at home. Dessert was berries from a nearby patch, eaten from our hands as we picked them. We both laughed at our stained lips and teeth.

As the sun went down, the air became chilly and Wynn threw more sticks on the fire. Then we wrapped ourselves in a blanket and sat with our backs to a large pine tree as we watched the stars begin to appear.

The evening was astir with the night life of the wilds. Wynn identified each sound for me—the cry of the loon, the swish from the wings of the mammoth owl as it swept earth-ward to snatch unsuspecting prey, a mouse scurrying through the pine needles, a bull moose bellowing out a challenge.

When the wolves began their evening chorus, I shivered some and was glad for Wynn's arm about me. But not even the wolves could disturb me on this night.

Everything would have been perfect if only we could have escaped the tormenting mosquitoes. Wynn threw green branches on the fire, and we sat in the smoke to hold them at bay.

As the sun totally disappeared, more stars twinkled into view, taking their appointed position in the velvet of the night sky.

And then it was that I saw the most spectacular sight of my entire life. Suddenly the sky was alive with sweeping rainbows. Lights swished and swirled above us, sweeping across the skies in spectacular movements. Sometimes the entire sky would seem to be one giant movement of color, and then the lights would retreat as though to end a scene, then sweep back again for another curtain call.

"They are so beautiful," I whispered wonderingly over and over, finding it hard to believe that it was just the north-ern lights we were watching. Though I had watched them in awe many times since coming north, I had never seen such a marvelous display.

We sat on through the evening, enjoying the night even after the last lights of our great northern fireworks faded from the skies. The deep blackness around us seemed to hem us in, promising protection. The stars shone even brighter as Wynn pointed out different constellations to me.

As I sat there in the warmth of Wynn's arms, I realized there might be many anniversaries stretching before us. I prayed to God that He would make it so. But there would never be one that could outshine the one we were sharing now.

August the first. I looked at the date on my calendar with some apprehension. I had seen Nimmie the evening before and she had looked fine. She had talked about their coming baby, her eyes gleaming. "Soon," she had said, "we will know if it will be a hunter or an herb-gatherer."

I managed to laugh at Nimmie's description of her boy or girl, but inside I felt a little twinge. Part of the twinge was nothing more than envy. I was still not with child and my daily prayers had not changed. The other part of the twinge was for Nimmie and her baby. The mortality rate among the Indian people was high, and I knew how much Nimmie wanted this baby. What a terrible thing if she were to be denied.

Again the thought surfaced that I would not be nearly as worried if it were I who was soon to deliver, for the mortality rate was not nearly as high among my people. It didn't even occur to me that a baby I carried might also be in danger at delivery. I just expected that when it was my turn, all would go well.

That was what Nimmie expected, too, I suddenly realized. She wasn't even considering the possibility of something going wrong.

And so I looked at the calendar with both trepidation and anticipation. In a short time we would know. What had the city doctor said? The fifth of August. The baby was due in only five more days.

I decided to drop in on Nimmie. I would bake a batch of bread as planned, have my prayer time and then go to see her.

My quiet time was longer than usual as I pleaded with God again for Nimmie's safe delivery—of the hunter or the herb-gatherer, I didn't care. When I was finished praying, I went to check on the rising bread. While it baked I turned my attention to some mending. Some buttons had been torn from Wynn's shirt when a trapper's unprovoked lead dog had ferociously attacked him. As I sewed, I was thankful that only the shirt had been damaged in the incident. I had to mend some little tears before I could replace the buttons, and by the time I was finished I could smell the aroma of freshly baked bread.

I carefully wrapped one loaf for Nimmie. I had just said no to Kip, who looked at me pleadingly, and reached for the loaf when there was a noise at the door. It was Mrs. Sam. She had not been to my house for some weeks.

I welcomed her in. Though I would be delayed now, I could not possibly tell Mrs. Sam that I was just leaving. She would expect her usual cup of tea.

I put the bread back on the table and pulled the teakettle forward on the stove. Thankfully the water was already hot. I made the tea and we sat and sipped it and ate sugar cookies while we chatted about village life.

Mrs. Sam said the berry prospects looked good. "Many, many," she stated and I was glad for that. I hoped to pick and preserve a number of jars of berries for our winter use. That along with our good garden would make the thought of another winter not nearly so dreary.

Mrs. Sam drank slowly while I fidgeted a bit. I was polite enough to offer a second cup of tea. Then a third. After the fourth, Mrs. Sam rose from her chair and pushed her cup back into the middle of the table.

"Nimmie say, 'Come now,' " she stated simply as my eves widened in surprise and horror. Nimmie had sent her to get me, and here we had sat sipping cup after cup of tea! I turned to grab the loaf of bread—though why, I'll never know—and hurried for the door. Mrs. Sam took her time following me.

I wanted to walk quickly—no, *run*—but Mrs. Sam kept her usual pace, which was unhurried and ambling. I wondered if it would be impolite for me to run on ahead.

"How is Nimmie?" I finally thought to ask, though I was a bit fearful of the answer.

"Good," answered Mrs. Sam.

"Is she—is she—?" I wasn't sure how to ask the question of an Indian woman with limited English. "Is she—in labor? Pain?"

"Nope."

"But she sent for me?" That wasn't like Nimmie.

"Yah."

"Was the midwife with her?"

"No more."

"No more?"

I couldn't understand it. Why would Nimmie send for me, and why would the midwife visit her and then leave? It all seemed very strange. And it was only August the first.

"Is Nimmie okay?" I asked again.

And Mrs. Sam's answer was the same as before. "Good."

"What about the baby?" I asked in exasperation.

"Her good, too."

I stopped in my tracks, trying to understand what Mrs. Sam had just said. She might have responded that way about an unborn child, but when the Indian women spoke of the unborn, they used the pronoun "him," not "her." Did that mean—surely not? But when I got my breath I asked anyway, "What do you mean, *her*?"

"Her," stated Mrs. Sam again as though it was clear enough. "Her. Girl baby."

After one wild look at Mrs. Sam I forgot to be polite any longer. I picked up my skirt and ran the rest of the way to Nimmie's cabin, causing the village dogs to nearly go mad on their tethers as I rushed.

Out of breath and trembling, I slowed down enough to rap gently on Nimmie's door; then without waiting for an answer, I pushed it open and walked in.

The small room of the cabin was filled with a strange odor, like nothing I had ever smelled before. I hurried to the bed in the corner, deciding the smell must be some herb medicine from the midwife.

And there was Nimmie, with a contented smile and a

small bundle with a red, wrinkled face held possessively on her arm.

"You said—you said August the fifth," I stammered.

"No," said Nimmie shaking her head and beaming at her new baby girl. "I said *the doctor* said August the fifth. Nonita did not wait for doctor's due. She came when she was ready."

I looked back to the tiny, beautiful baby in Nimmie's arms. A prayer arose in my heart. She was here, and she was safe, and she was about the prettiest thing I had ever seen.

"A little herb-gatherer," I said with tears in my eyes. "Oh, Nimmie, she's beautiful!"

Chapter Nine

Nonita

I stood for many minutes looking down at Nimmie's tiny new baby girl. Her dainty curled fists lay in a relaxed position on her chubby cheeks, her dark hair slightly curled over her forehead. Her eyes were closed and just a trace of eyelash showed because of the slight puffiness due to her recent arrival. I had proclaimed her beautiful. There may be those who would have argued with me. A newborn is really not too beautiful. But she was healthy and whole, and given a few days to adjust to her new world, I knew she would look beautiful. I felt a twinge within me again—that something which told me that just at this moment, Nimmie was one of the most blessed people I knew.

I suddenly returned to reality. "When did she arrive?" I asked Nimmie.

"About an hour ago. I think the clock said 10:45."

It was now ten minutes to twelve.

"What does Ian think of having a daughter?" I asked, not because I needed to ask but because I thought Nimmie might wish to express it.

"He still doesn't know," said Nimmie, a bit of impatience in her voice.

"Doesn't *know*?" It was incredulous to me that Ian had not been informed.

"He went to the woods with the men this morning to fell some more trees for the trading post."

"But—" I began.

"He left at six," Nimmie went on.

"Didn't you know—?" I started to ask, but Nimmie interrupted.

"Yes," she said hesitantly. "I thought, but I didn't want to keep him from his work."

"Oh, Nimmie!" I said. "Don't you know Ian would have wanted to be here? The logs can wait, but your baby—"

"Yes, babies won't wait," said Nimmie. "I learned that much. I told the midwife I wanted to wait until Ian got home. He said he would be here shortly after midday. But, Nonita— well, she wouldn't wait."

I looked again at the clock. If Ian said he would be back soon after noon, he should be coming any time now. I heaved a sigh of relief and turned back to Nimmie.

"Would you like anything? Soup? Tea?"

"The midwife gave me some of her birthing herbs," she said. "I feel just fine. A little tired, but just fine."

Nonita suddenly squirmed in Nimmie's arms and screwed up her face. She began to cry, her face growing even more red. She had not yet developed the lusty cry of an older infant. Nimmie adjusted her on her arm and held her to nurse, crooning comforting words to her in her own native tongue.

The baby stopped her fussing and snuggled up against Nimmie. The deep red drained from her face. Nimmie cradled her and then began to sing her an Indian lullaby.

I discovered I was still carrying my loaf of bread, somewhat misshapen due to my run. I wanted to laugh at its ridiculous shape now, but I was afraid I might disturb Nimmie or the baby, so I crossed as quietly as I could and placed it on the table.

Nimmie's song soon ended. She looked at me, her eyes still shining.

"That is the song my mother used to sing to me. Perhaps

every Indian baby has listened to that song. I will sing it to all my children as well."

"It's a pretty song," I said, crossing the room to her bedside.

"It speaks of the forests, the rivers, the moon in the sky, and promises the baby that all of nature will be her new home."

"That's nice." I touched her arm and smiled at her precious bundle.

Nimmie closed her eyes. I didn't know if she was visualizing her child in the years to come or if she was just tired.

"Nimmie, perhaps you should rest now. Would you like me to stay or to leave?"

"There's no need for you to stay, Elizabeth. Ian will soon be here. I sent for you because I was anxious for you to see Nonita. It wasn't because I did not want to be alone."

"I don't mind staying."

"I'm fine—really."

"Then I will go and let you rest."

I was about to leave when she looked up at me and smiled. "Would you like to hold Nonita before you go?"

I didn't even answer; my heart was too full and my throat too tight. I reached down for the sleeping baby as Nimmie lifted her gently toward my outstretched hands.

She was so little and so light in my arms that I felt as if I were holding only a dream, only a fairy child. She opened one squinty little eye and seemed to wink at me. It was an uncontrolled action I knew, but I laughed anyway.

"She's beautiful," I declared again, and I meant it with all of my heart.

I laid the baby on the bed beside her mother. Nimmie smiled contentedly.

"Someday, Elizabeth," she said, "it will be your turn—and then you will know the deep river of happiness flowing within me now."

Chapter Ten

Summer

Nimmie was soon back on her feet. Even with her new baby she still found time to work in her garden and tend the store and manage the other tasks she had been used to doing. I tried to help some, but she usually caught me at it and laughed at my concern.

"I am as strong as ever, Elizabeth," she assured me. "Where do you white women get the idea that having a child makes one weak and unable to do one's own work?"

So we went to the garden together and hoed the weeds and pulled the vegetables for use on our tables. We opened the store and cared for the customers who came for supplies. We even went to the berry patches together, with Nonita secured to Nimmie's back, and sometimes I got to carry her for short distances.

Nonita gradually lost her redness and puffiness. She did not lose her swatch of dark thick hair nor her black, black eyes, however. Ian adored her. Even Wynn seemed captured by the little one. I would gladly have babysat, but Nimmie never seemed to need anyone to care for the tiny girl.

The trading post building was coming along nicely. Rain storms no longer delayed its progress, for there was still much to be done inside the structure. The rooms at the back were also being worked on, and Nimmie began to show her eagerness to be in and settled. This attitude was new to Nimmie, who was normally so patient and placid about everything. I suppose having the baby made her want to be in her own home rather than the makeshift cabin.

I scarcely saw Wynn these days except at night. He was usually gone before I awakened in the morning. He wanted to cover all his distant rounds before the first snowfall in a month or so.

After a morning in a berry patch or the nearby woods, the Indian ladies often came in the afternoon for their cup of tea. I was glad to resume our visits. We still didn't spend all our time talking, though I did understand many more Indian words; but there were comfortable times of sitting together just sipping tea and smiling at one another.

Kip's injuries from his fight with Buck had healed nicely. He seemed to have become a bit cocky, however, and I was sure he would never back down to any dog in the future. Whenever I went into the settlement, I left him at home or put him on the leash Wynn had provided. I did not wish a dog fight every time I went to the village, even if Kip should turn out to be the victor.

During the month of August three more babies were born in the village, but only one of them lived. There was great mourning among the people as the tiny graves were dug. I sorrowed too, thinking of the mothers and the pain they must feel.

The days became noticeably shorter, and we knew summer would not be with us forever.

Chapter Eleven

Another Winter

With the honking of the Canada geese and the autumn dance of the leaves in the blustery winds, we knew fall was here. The berry patches had been stripped of all of their fruit. We had either canned the berries or else dried them in the sun.

Wynn was working a little closer to the settlement now, and I was up in time to prepare his breakfast each morning before he went to another day's work.

The welcome day arrived when Nimmie moved from the cramped cabin to her new home. I insisted on the enjoyable task of caring for Nonita while Nimmie settled in with the nesting instinct of a mother robin. When I reluctantly returned the precious little bundle, Nimmie chirped and twittered to her little nestling and Nonita smiled and gurgled back.

I often noticed the Indian men studying the sky. Even the women, as they walked to the nearby woods for their daily wood supply for their fires, glanced heavenward as though the skies held many answers to the days that lay ahead.

I wanted to keep the Indian summer forever. I was not happy about the thought of being shut in again by the swirling snow and the howling winds. I was sure Wynn was not looking forward to the difficult days of winter either, but he made no comment.

Kip's fur grew thicker and fluffier and I knew the wild animals, too, were wearing a warmer coat against the cold that was to come. I no longer heard the birds fighting over the scraps of produce left in my garden. Most of them had already migrated south.

And then one morning when I rose from my warm bed, I noticed a chill about the house, even though Wynn had already started the fire in the stove. My glance went to the window and I saw the snow gently sifting down. If I had not been dreading it so, I would have most surely thought it to be beautiful. It fell in large, soft flakes, and as it floated gently on the slight wind, it looked like fluffy down. After my time in the North, I knew better, so I did not stop to enjoy the sight. Instead, I went into Wynn's office to draw some consolation from him.

"It's snowing," I informed him as soon as I reached his door.

He looked up from the dog harness he was mending and nodded.

"It's only October," I complained, as though Wynn should know better than to let it snow so early.

"I know," he answered. "It likely won't last for long."

I knew he was trying to reassure me. I also knew that some years the snow *did* come to stay even in October. I hoped this wouldn't be one of those years.

I looked at what Wynn was doing. The dog harnesses were only used when there was snow on the ground.

He noticed my accusing gaze.

"Didn't have anything else that needed doing this morning," he explained defensively, "so I thought I might as well get an early start on this."

I nodded and changed the subject. "I'll have breakfast in a few minutes," I said, and turned back to the little kitchen area and the singing kettle.

The snow fell all that day, and the next and the next. *We*

won't be seeing the last of it for some time, I groaned silently.

I was feeling close to despair when there was a knock on my door. Nimmie came in, shaking the snow from her bare head and the blankets covering Nonita.

I was surprised to see her, but I shouldn't have been. A little thing like a few inches of snow would not have kept Nimmie home.

"I have some good news," she said, even before she un-wrapped the baby and removed her coat.

She didn't wait for me to ask but went on, "Remember I said that Ian had to pay a visit to the main village?"

I nodded, reaching for the squirming Nonita.

"Well, he's back. I asked him to check with the chief about us starting a school. He did, and the chief just shrugged his shoulders and said that if we wanted to teach the children letters, it was up to us, just as long as we didn't interfere with their rightful duties. We can go ahead, Elizabeth; we can start our classes! Now that winter seems to be here the children will be free to attend for a few hours each day."

We could go ahead and start our school! So the snow had brought some good. I looked out the window as my heart thanked God for the welcome news.

I turned back to Nimmie, the small Nonita still in my arms. "Oh, Nimmie!" I exclaimed, "we have so much to do to get ready! So much planning. Where will we hold it and—?"

Nimmie laughed and reclaimed her baby. "Slow down, Elizabeth," she said; "we'll get it all worked out."

I made the tea and Nimmie sat down at my table. We got pencils and paper and began to work through every part of our plan.

I would do the actual teaching. Nimmie would be my helper and interpreter as needed. We planned to pool our resources for classroom supplies. Ian could send out for some pencils and scribblers for the students' use. He had another wagon train due in soon with the winter supplies for the settlement. The carrier was leaving in two days with the additions to Ian's supply list, so our needs would have to be figured out and presented to Ian very quickly.

My mind could hardly work in the excitement. Another of my prayers had been answered: We would get our school.

Chapter Twelve

School

Even though Nimmie and I went right to work on our plans and materials for the new school, still it was near the end of November before we held our first class.

That first early snow had not left us. Instead, it had been added to by three separate storms. Wynn now used his sled dogs for his rounds, and the snow was almost deep enough for snowshoes. Many of the village men already had left the comfort of the village and returned to their traplines.

My only consolation for the early winter was the proposed school. Even with the chief's approval, we knew our classes would have to be kept short. The children were needed to gather the family's wood supply and carry water from the river. It had not frozen over yet but would soon, and then daily a hole would have to be cut in the ice in order for them to dip out the necessary water. When the ice got too thick, the settlement families would have to simply melt the drifted snow.

I was glad we had a well with a pump. The villagers were welcome to use it, but most of them declared pumping a "bad job," as the small stream of water took a long time to fill their pail. In the summer months some of the children liked to play with the pump. They usually came together, two or three boys, and not too much of the pumped water ever found its way to the village home. Most of it remained in puddles in our yard, or soaked through the boys' clothing.

Nimmie and I planned for classes from nine to twelve. It didn't seem like much, but we thought it better to take it easy than to overdo and have parents complaining about school keeping the youngsters from their duties.

A classroom was one of our biggest problems. I knew our cabin was too small. We would be able to fit only eight at the most. We were hoping for a better attendance than that. We considered the empty Lamuir cabin Nimmie and Ian had used. It also was small, but with simple tables and benches, it might give us enough room for now. We discussed this with our husbands, and they made plans to have the tables and benches made.

We also needed a wood supply for the fireplace in the cabin. Wynn took care of that; with three or four men, he went to the nearby wood and hauled out dead, fallen logs. The logs were brought to the village and cut into proper lengths for our fireplace, then stacked up against the side of the small cabin.

We had no way to advertise our classes, so Nimmie and I walked from door to door, telling each household about our plan. Many of the people had no clocks, only the sun and their uncanny but rather accurate sense of time. Nimmie borrowed the idea of the store-hour signal, which was no longer in effect, Ian having taken over regular hours since his new building was useable. So as we went from door to door, we told them to listen for the banging of the hammer on the drum barrel, and then they would know that school was to begin.

Both Wynn and Ian supported us completely in our project. Many times as Nimmie and I worked over our lesson plans, one or the other would offer advice.

"If you want to get their attention and make them interested in learning," offered Wynn, "then you must teach them things that relate to their life. No 'c-a-t spells cat.' " (We had no cats in the village. The dogs would have torn them to shreds.)

"Use words they know: fish, canoe, river, forest, dog, moon, sun, stars, trap."

I could see what Wynn was getting at and I agreed with him, at least until we fully had introduced learning to our students. We did hope also to expand the world as they knew it.

We had few textbooks. The scribblers and pencils arrived with the winter supplies. As a surprise for Nimmie and me, Ian had also ordered a small chalkboard and a good supply of chalk with two brushes. We were thrilled with it all. When Wynn mounted the chalkboard on a wall in the cabin, it looked like a real classroom.

One further problem was lack of light. The cabin's one tiny window afforded little illumination even on the brightest of days, and much less during the dreary winter months. Ian gave us the use of two oil lamps from the store, but even they did not light up our little room very well.

But Nonita was not a problem—she was a contented baby, who still slept many hours of her life away, and Nimmie would be able to bring her to school and care for her as necessary.

Since we were beginning with words and concepts the Indian children knew, I needed teaching material. I wanted pictures to accompany the words. I had none. I was not an artist, but I set to work trying to illustrate the words on the cards I had made. "Fish" was not difficult, and my "canoe" and "sled" were recognizable, but "dog" and "deer" and "moose" required a lot of imagination.

I wasn't sure how to show the difference between the sun and the moon. Did the Indian people see the moon with a smiling face? As I labored over my drawings, I certainly recognized their inadequacies. I wasn't sure if my "art" would help or hinder my students' progress.

At last the long-awaited day arrived. Wynn promised to build our fire and have the chill out of the cabin by the time the teachers and the students arrived. I gathered the rest of my teaching tools together, bundled myself up against the cold wind, closed the door on the whining Kip, and headed for the exciting first day of school.

Nimmie was already there. The room was cozy and warm. The crude tables and chairs were the best that could be managed out of rough lumber, and I knew they held the possibility of many future slivers. Beneath our blackboard was a piece of chalk and one of our brushes. A few of my books were on a shelf along with our supply of scribblers and the pencils Wynn carefully had sharpened for us with his jackknife.

I had thought that supplies were quite limited in my schoolhouse at Pine Spring, and so they were; but here at the settlement I had even less to work with and just as great a need.

We were ready. This was our school. I took a deep breath and smiled at Nimmie, giving her the nod to "ring our bell."

I don't know if I really expected a stampede to our door. If I did, I certainly shouldn't have. I knew the Indian people better than that, and yet somehow because of my own great excitement, I guess I expected them to be excited too.

At the end of our gonging signal, we waited for our first student. No one came. The minutes ticked by, and still no one showed up.

I began to feel panicky, but Nimmie seemed perfectly at ease. She threw another log in the fireplace, then crossed over to where tiny Nonita was sleeping on a bear rug in the corner and sat down beside her on the floor.

"Do you think we should bang on it again?" I asked anxiously.

"They heard," said Nimmie.

I too was sure they had heard. One could not have lived anywhere in the village and not have heard the terrible din of the clanging barrel ringing out over the crisp morning air.

We waited.

"Why aren't they coming?" I asked Nimmie.

"They'll come," Nimmie assured me, unperturbed.

We waited some more.

Nimmie was right. At last two girls came toward the cabin. I, who had been watching out the window for any sign of activity, met them at the door. I wanted to be sure they didn't change their minds.

Three more girls, hiding giggles behind their hands, soon followed, and then another, and then four boys, grouped together as if for support. Two more girls, a single, a pair of boys. They kept straggling in until I feared that most of our morning would be taken with trying to get some kind of a roll call established.

I welcomed the children and found them each a place to sit. Nimmie repeated my words in their own native tongue. I explained to them what we would be doing at school, hoping the excitement in my voice would somehow carry over to them. Twenty-three pairs of eyes never left my face, but I saw no flicker of interest or enthusiasm. I swallowed hard and went on.

"We will be learning numbers and words and colors," I continued, trying to make it sound fascinating, but the expressions before me did not change.

Nimmie stepped forward to stand beside me. She began to speak to them in her own soft and flowing speech. I understood only a few of the words, but somehow they managed to convey to me, and to the children, a sense of wonder—an inspiration. A few eyes before me began to light.

As we worked on the roll call, other stragglers arrived. Our schoolhouse was crowded. We didn't have room to seat any more. I was exhilarated! *Wait till I tell Wynn!* I exulted. I remembered his words of caution.

"Don't be too disappointed, Elizabeth, if you have very few students. The value system of the people here varies greatly from ours. They do not see the need, or the advantage, of spending many hours trying to learn about things they will never see nor know. What good is all that learning if it will not put food in the pot, or coax the fox to the trap?"

And here we were with a full schoolhouse! Wouldn't Wynn be surprised?

About midway through the morning two women arrived, chattering as they entered and looking over the room full of children and each item in it. They discussed freely what they observed. I guess they had never been told that one does not talk without permission in a school setting. They found a place on the floor and sat down.

Later on more women joined them, singly or by twos or threes. I could hardly believe it! Our schoolroom was packed full of eager and willing learners—of all ages. We would need more room, more pencils and scribblers. I hadn't thought of teaching the women, but of course they needed it too.

Nimmie did not seem surprised. She only nodded a greeting to each one as they came and motioned them to a still-vacant spot on the floor.

I decided to concentrate on the children and let the women learn by listening and observing, so I did not put any of the adult names in my roll book.

After getting the names of the students recorded, which took a great deal of help from Nimmie, I proceeded with my first lesson. Taking my cards with the words and pictures, I held them aloft and pointed first at a picture and then at the English word. I said the word over two or three times and then Nimmie told the students to say the word with me. We went over it a number of times. *Canoe. Canoe. Canoe.* Then we went on to the the next one. *Fish. Fish. Fish.* I had the class say it together and then picked out students to try it on their own. They were shy about it, hesitant to make a funny-sounding word in front of others, so I went back to having them say it together.

I took the two new words now and covered the pictures.

"What does this say?" I asked them, and Nimmie repeated my question.

No one knew. I uncovered the picture and asked the question again. They replied correctly almost in unison.

We went over the two words again and again, and still

they did not seem to recognize them when the pictures were covered.

At last when I covered the picture and held one up, a small boy said, "Canoe." He was right and I was ecstatic. There was whispering in the row where the boy sat and I saw Nimmie's face crinkle with laughter.

I couldn't refrain from asking, "What did he say?"

"His classmate asked him how he knew the picture, and he said the canoe card has a small tear at one corner," explained Nimmie.

I looked down at the picture. He was right.

It set me back some, but then I realized it did prove he was observant and intelligent. Those ingredients made a scholar. I just had to find the right approach, that was all.

I switched from the word cards to colors. I was aware that the Indians know much about color. They just don't know what the white man calls them. The color lesson did not go well either. Every time I pointed to a color on an object, they thought I was asking for the name of the object, not the color.

Nimmie explained to them, and things went a bit better. After much drilling, I was quite confident a good number in the class had learned "black" and "white."

We dismissed them, telling them to hurry back to the schoolroom the next morning when they heard the bell clang. I didn't know if our admonition would avail or not. Most likely they would come when they felt ready.

The students began to file out, some looking thankful for freedom. The women still sat on the floor. It appeared they didn't intend to leave, and I thrilled with their interest in learning. I told Nimmie to express to them my happiness at seeing them at school and my promise to do my best to help them learn. Nimmie passed on my information in a flow of words, but the blank look on the women's faces did not change.

Little Deer said what all of them must have been thinking. "When tea?"

We tried our best to explain that we didn't serve tea at

school, and with looks of disappointment, they got up and filed out one by one.

I felt exhausted after the first morning. Nimmie looked as fresh and relaxed as ever, and little Nonita had roused only once, nursed and gone back to sleep.

I gathered up my word cards, looked at the canoe to see if I might be able to fix the tear, abandoned the idea, and headed for home.

I honestly did not know if our first day at school had been a success or not. We certainly had a roomful of students. But if they did not learn, was it worth their time to be sitting there? I decided not to do too much bragging to Wynn as yet.

Chapter Thirteen

The Three R's

We banged the barrel the next morning and again waited for our students to return. The room was not as full as it had been the previous day, but I was not concerned. I knew that as the morning progressed more students would arrive. I didn't expect any of the ladies. They had felt cheated out of a tea party and would stay home beside their fires.

When Wynn had asked about our first day, I could not refrain from boasting some about the numbers. Wynn just nodded encouragement without comment and I wondered if he was saying silently, "Elizabeth, don't set yourself up for a heartbreak."

I'm not sure why I felt that way, except that I was getting to know the way Wynn thought. The expression in his eyes often said things he didn't put into words.

More students did straggle in as the morning went on. We went back to our two words of the day before. Everyone could now pick out the canoe once they had been given the secret of the torn corner. A few even recognized "fish"—without a tear on the card.

I went on to another word. "Dog," I said, holding high the card. Nimmie announced the Indian word for dog and then repeated it in English. There was a bit of tittering in the

classroom and black eyes flashed secret messages of merri-
ment. I turned to Nimmie.

"They think it looks more like a skinny bear," she informed me with a slight smile.

I looked back at my picture. It certainly wasn't a very
good dog. I didn't dare show them my deer or moose. I went
on to the moon and the sun. They seemed to have some difficulty with these concepts as well.

I tacked the cards to the wall and told them to open their
scribblers, take a pencil and copy the words in their book.

They were not clumsy naturally; in fact, they were unu-
sually dexterous, but how to hold a pencil posed a good deal
of difficulty at first. Many of Wynn's carefully sharpened
points were broken in the attempt.

Nimmie and I circulated among them, showing them how
to hold the pencil properly and how much pressure to put on
the point. I laid aside all the pencils needing to be resharp-
ened to take home to Wynn and his jackknife.

Most of the students got "fish" and "canoe" entered in
their new scribblers, though some of the attempts were hardly
recognizable.

I was surprised that some of the women did join us again,
even though they knew that tea was not forthcoming. They
settled themselves on the floor and appeared to listen—
whether out of curiosity or interest, I did not know.

As I went quietly from student to student, I was surprised
by a boy of about twelve or thirteen. Not only had he printed
his words, and rather neatly at that, but he had also drawn
the pictures. It didn't take a teaching certificate to see that
his pictures were far superior to mine. I hastened to Nimmie,
excitement filling me.

"Come here," I whispered. "Look what he's done."

The "he" was Wawasee. His father was a trapper, one of
those whose trapline was some miles from the village. The
mother had died in childbirth two years previously. Wawasee
was left each winter to care for himself and two younger
sisters. Had he been alone, he undoubtedly would have been

taken out to the trapline, but two small girls out there would be more bother than help. I learned from Nimmie that Wawasee spent much of his time carving wood with a dull, broken knife that had somehow come into his possession.

My heart reached out to this boy. He was dirty and unkempt, but his dark eyes glistened as he printed each word on the page and stroked in the pencil marks to skillfully create a picture. *I must talk to Wynn about Wawasee*, I determined.

At the end of the morning session we dismissed our students and instructed them to leave their pencils and scribblers on the tables as they filed out. We would ring the "bell" at the same time the next morning.

My interest in Wawasee was undoubtedly the reason I noticed that his scribbler and pencil did not stay behind. I had been so anxious to take it home to show Wynn.

I looked around to see if it had been misplaced, but I did not spot it. I gathered up each of the other scribblers and placed them back on the shelf, still glancing under tables and benches. Nimmie noticed it.

"Did you lose something?" she asked.

"Wawasee's scribbler. It isn't here."

"I'm not surprised," remarked Nimmie.

I looked at her questioningly.

"Wawasee cannot hear," she stated simply. "He lip reads some, but I was not standing where he could see me when I repeated your instructions."

"Oh, Nimmie," was all I could say.

"But even if he had been able to hear the order, I don't think Wawasee would have left his book," Nimmie went on in a quiet voice.

"Is he a . . . a . . ." I couldn't say the word *thief*. It just didn't seem to fit the child, and besides I didn't want to think of him in that way.

"Wawasee uses anything he finds to make pictures," Nimmie explained. "He draws them in the dirt, on birchbark; he scratches them on tree trunks. And you have just passed to him a scribbler and a pencil. What would you expect him to do?"

"He'll draw?"

"He'll probably have half the pages full by morning."

I stood rooted to the spot, thinking of the little Indian boy, with a full-grown man's responsibility, no hearing, and a great talent for art.

"Would you like me to go and get the scribbler?" Nimmie was asking.

I turned back to her. "No," I said, "but I would like to talk to the boy. Could you come with me? I don't know how to make him understand me."

Nimmie agreed, and we tramped our way through the softly swirling snow of another winter storm to the unkempt cabin of the boy and his two little sisters.

Nimmie opened the door and went in, and there, just as she expected to find him, was Wawasee. His concentration was totally taken with the pencil in his hand and the picture forming beneath it. He was not aware of our presence in the cabin as he sketched a moose running through the dense undergrowth, a wolf fast on its heels.

Nimmie crossed to him and laid her hand on his arm. He looked up in surprise and then alarm. Slowly he slid the scribbler off the table and hid it on his lap as if to protect it. His eyes were dark and pleading. I thought of Kip when he wanted to go someplace with me.

Nimmie smiled and some of the fear left Wawasee's eyes.

Somehow Nimmie was able to tell the boy that I wanted him to draw the pictures on the word cards for the class. In exchange for his work for me, he would be given a pencil and a scribbler all his own—one that would not need to go to school but that he could keep at home to use whenever he wished.

I knew that through lip reading and sign language, he understood all Nimmie had said, for he looked at me, back to his pencil, down at his lap, and nodded, his eyes shining with unshed tears.

Chapter Fourteen

Trials and Triumphs

At the end of our first week of school, we were down to thirteen students. At first I pretended they had some reason which kept them from the morning class. Nimmie knew better. She did not even seem surprised. Instead, she said with excitement, "Thirteen. Elizabeth! Thirteen. Can you believe it? We still have *thirteen* who are interested."

I wanted to argue with her. Thirteen was only about half of what we had started with.

By the end of the second week our number had dropped to five. Just five—when there was a village full of people who needed to learn to read and write. Nimmie was still not alarmed. "Five for our first year is wonderful. In the years to come the others will see the importance of knowing how to read, too."

I hoped Nimmie was right, but I will admit I was terribly disappointed.

Our remaining five included Wawasee our artist, a young lad by the name of Jim Buck, two girls—one eight, one eleven—and a young married woman who came with her nursing baby. The young mother would often get so involved in what she was learning that she would forget the child in her arms. The fussing baby eventually would bring her back to reality, and she would lift the baby to her breast and go back to her book again. I had never seen anyone so eager to learn as Brown Duck.

Kanika, our eleven-year-old, was not a quick learner, but she had a searching mind and would plod away to find the answers to the problems we assigned her.

Susie Crooked Leg, on the other hand, was a brilliant little child. She rarely had to be told a new concept twice. Eagerly she grasped all the learning the small classroom was able to give her and reached for more. I knew that if Susie could be given a chance, she could make a real contribution to her world and even beyond.

Wawasee was at a disadvantage. We had nothing in our classroom that could help a child with his handicap. He had not been born deaf but had been a bright, energetic, talkative, eight-year-old when measles left him without his hearing. We had to be sure we were directly in front of him with his eyes on our lips when we talked to him. This was not always easy to do, for Wawasee was interested only in his drawing. He drew when he should have been reading. He was not interested in numbers or letters, only shapes and colors.

I was determined that he at least should learn the fundamentals. I prompted and urged and reviewed and encouraged. Once, when he had been at school for about a week and the other students had gone on to add a number of simple words to their vocabulary, Wawasee was still struggling with the first two.

"Fish," I would say over and over, enunciating carefully for the benefit of his eyes on my lips. "Fish."

Wawasee tried the word. It sounded good.

I then put him to work printing the word over and over down his page. I even granted him the privilege of drawing a small fish to go with each of the words. After he had filled two pages with fish of various sizes and descriptions, I went to the board and with a piece of white chalk, printed in large letters F-I-S-H. After getting Wawasee's attention, I asked him for the word.

He shook his head. He did not know.

I was frustrated. I walked back to his desk and opened the scribbler to the two pages of fish. Placing a finger under Wawasee's chin, a signal we had developed to let him know we wanted him to watch our lips, I said again, "Fish. It is the same. Fish." I pointed to the board, "F-I-S-H." I pointed to his pages. "The same," but Wawasee merely shrugged his shoulders.

Lifting his eyes to my face again, I asked gently, "Do you understand?"

He looked at me evenly, as though asking me to see it his way, "Not same," he dared to say. "Yours white, mine black."

Wawasee thought in color.

I realized then that I needed a new way to relate to Wawasee. If only I had many bright books with colored pages. Perhaps then he would be interested in learning. But I did not have them, and it would be months before it would be possible to get some. In the meantime I would simply do the best I could.

One of my disappointments was that Wawasee's two younger sisters did not come to school. I asked Wawasee about them many times. At first his answer, through Nimmie's translation, was that they were not interested in drawing. When we reminded him that school was so much more than that, he looked for other answers. Each time we asked him, his reply was a little different, but it all came down to the fact that the little girls just were not interested and did not feel that classes were sufficient reason to leave the sheltered warmth of the cabin.

After the fourth week Kanika dropped out. I felt like crying. I went to their cabin after school was dismissed hoping to learn that she had been ill or needed at home. She was fine and was playing rather than doing an assigned home task. Her mother just shrugged her shoulders.

"Why you not go?" she asked the girl in English for my benefit, as though she had just realized that Kanika was at home and not at school.

Kanika barely raised her head to answer. She looked puzzled, as though she couldn't understand why she should be called upon to explain herself. It was plain to see that she just didn't feel like going, so she didn't go—that was all.

Now we had four students. Wawasee was hardly to be counted, for though we worked with him to the best of our ability, his attention was on his artwork only.

Jim Buck, Susie Crooked Leg and Brown Duck were doing well. All three were eager to learn.

Then we had another disappointment. Brown Duck's husband came home from his trapline for a few days and learned of her involvement in the classes. He could not understand her hunger for knowledge. He only knew that she was the only woman in the settlement who was leaving her work at home to go to class each morning. He could also see that skins were not getting tanned, moccasins were not getting sewn, and the cabin fire was not kept burning.

We could understand the attitude of Crying Dog, Brown Duck's husband. He saw the schooling as a waste of time for a lazy wife and he forbade Brown Duck to return to class again.

We were sorry to lose Brown Duck, but neither Nimmie nor I would have encouraged her to disobey her husband.

It was no longer reasonable to expect Nimmie to come to the schoolroom each morning when I had only three students. The students and I understood one another well enough now that we could manage. I had a little of their language, they were learning more and more words in English. I knew they should learn English, because they needed it to communicate outside their own small world; but I was sorry they were unable to have textbooks in their native tongue. They should have had the privilege of learning their own language in written form, but at this point they did not.

The weather grew colder, the winds blew more drifts of snow, tucking our little village in blankets of white. We needed snowshoes to get about. The women of the village were kept constantly busy supplying fuel for their cabin fires.

I was wrestling with a question. Was it sensible to have Wynn go to the little cabin each morning and start a fire for just the four of us? Wouldn't it make more sense to move my students over to my cabin for their lessons? But if I stayed where I was, there might be those who would return to class. I finally talked it over with Wynn.

"What should I do?" I asked him after I had thoroughly explained my predicament.

"I would like to believe that there might be those who will rejoin you, Elizabeth," he said slowly, "but to be honest, I don't suppose they will. They have had no reason to believe that education from books will benefit them. That still has to be proven to them."

"But how can we show them?" I wailed.

"We can't—not overnight. It is going to take a long time. Perhaps," he went on thoughtfully, "we are a negative example to them."

"Negative? I don't follow."

"Well, I have education. You have education. And yet we need to learn their skills to live here in their wilderness."

I began to understand what Wynn was saying. I looked out our frosted window at the swirl of the winter storm. Wynn was right. Here my teaching degree would benefit me very little unless I also knew the art of survival.

"What should I do, Wynn?" I asked again, sincerely, humbly.

He reached out and pulled me into his arms. He smiled into my eyes as he stroked back the whisp of hair forever tormenting me by curling about my cheeks and refusing to stay combed in its proper place. "You're doing a great job," he said, "and I'm proud of you for trying, for caring. You might not realize it yet, but those two pupils of yours, just those two eager learners—yes, even Wawasee too—could someday be the means of educating this entire village."

I closed my eyes and leaned hard against my husband. With all my heart I hoped he was right.

Chapter Fifteen

Another Christmas

For some reason I dreaded the coming Christmas away from family even more than I had my first one. Perhaps it was because on my first year away I was still a new bride with the excitement of creating a home for my husband. Now I was beginning to notice the loneliness of the months without family. The coming of Christmas made me feel even more homesick.

I did not go crying to Wynn. He had enough troubles of his own. Reports were coming in from the traplines about a marauding bear robbing the traps. At first Wynn found the rumors hard to believe. All the bears should have been in hibernation months earlier. Whatever would one be doing out, still foraging for food, this time of year? The reports persisted. Wynn decided he must check into them.

According to those who brought the tales to the village, the bear was mammoth. It swung deadly blows with paws the size of pine branches and was gone again before a hunter could even lift his rifle. Soon other details were added to the stories. The bear was ten feet tall, bullets would not pierce him, and when he ran he left no tracks. The people of the village were sure the bear was a spirit animal and that it had come back to avenge some wrong, hitherto undetected. So afraid had they become that when Wynn decided to go out after "the spirit bear," he could find no one willing to go with him.

I don't know if some of the Indians' superstitions affected me, or what was the true nature of my despair, but I pleaded with Wynn not to go. I was sure that if he did, I would never see him again.

Wynn tried to assure me that he would be fine and would soon be home again, but I still feared for his life. He did not let this sway his decision, however. Already two trappers had been attacked by the bear. One had lost a leg in the attack and the other was mauled badly about the head and face.

The bear had also attacked sled dogs. It had killed one outright, another had to be destroyed because of a serious injury, and a third one seemed to be slowly healing. I knew Wynn was right, that something had to be done, but how I hated to see him leave on the trail of the killer bear.

"Something is wrong," Wynn said to me. "There are too many stories for me to doubt, but why a bear should be up and about this time of year is a mystery."

With a tear-stained face I watched Wynn fill his pack with an extra large emergency supply. I had seen him pack many times during our time spent up North, and I realized he was preparing for a long time on the trail, if necessary. I was even more frightened.

After watching Wynn and the dog team disappear from view through the swirling snow, I went back to my room and cried some more. *Perhaps this Christmas I won't even have Wynn*, I mourned.

When I awoke after crying myself to sleep, I felt worse, not better. My head ached and my eyes were swollen and sore. My throat felt sore, too, and I thought I might be coming down with something dreadful. *What if Wynn comes back to a cold cabin and lifeless wife?* But, no, that was foolishness. I really was letting my imagination run away with me.

If only the cabin didn't feel so empty when Wynn was gone. I thought again of the baby I wanted so badly. I had been married for almost a year and a half, and I still had no prospects of becoming a mother. Nimmie, who already had one little one, was already expecting another. Every day that I went to the settlement, I saw young women who were with child. It was a sad reminder to me that my arms were still empty. I shivered in the stillness and then suddenly realized that I had a good reason to shiver: It was cold in the cabin. I pulled myself from the bed and went to rebuild a fire.

I had prepared myself emotionally for many long, long days without Wynn. But by lunchtime the next day he was back. On the sled was tied the carcass of the largest bear I had ever seen. Though it was big, it was gaunt and empty, like it had already been skinned out and only the hide remained. One of its front paws was badly damaged, which, Wynn said, was the reason for our trouble.

"It couldn't hunt with that damaged paw and was starving slowly. It refused to go into hibernation without having the fat stored up to see it through the winter, so it stayed out to hunt. But it still had trouble finding enough to eat. Ordinarily it wouldn't have attacked dogs or men, but this bear was desperate."

I was so glad to see Wynn back that I didn't pay much attention to the bear. The Indian people did, though. They kept circling the sled, pointing at the carcass and talking in excited tones. They noticed the gaunt body, the visible ribs, the weakness of the big frame. They took it as an omen. It was not good, they said, that "brother bear" went hungry. Perhaps he was sent by the Great Spirit to warn of coming hunger for the people as well.

It was not a nice thought, and I will admit it made shivers run up and down my spine. Wynn seemed to pay no attention to the clucking tongues and shaking heads, but I do think he began to wish he had left that bear where he had shot it, instead of bringing it back to the settlement to prove to the people that it was no ghost.

Now that Wynn was safely back and the bear had been taken care of, I again gave my attention to Christmas. Actually I tried not to think about it, but I could not help myself.

I tried to keep myself busy so I wouldn't have time to think, but that didn't work either.

Two days before Christmas, Wynn came home in the morning to find the students and me poring over our books. He looked rather surprised and apologized for interrupting us. I assured him he had not troubled us and dismissed my students early.

"Aren't you even going to take a Christmas break?" Wynn inquired when the students had left for the day.

"Of course," I answered, as though Christmas were still far in the future. And then I remembered I hadn't told the students not to return the next morning, the twenty-fourth. *Well, I can't help it*, I reasoned. I just couldn't bear to spend the days alone.

Even when I worked, my thoughts kept going home. I remembered the Christmases spent with my family in Toronto. I could visualize just what preparations my mother would be making. I could see her, bending over her stove, her cheeks flushed from the warmth, her hair curling softly about her cheeks as she turned out pan after pan of delicious-smelling cookies. I could see Father as he entered the room with the fine tree, smelling as tangy as the very outdoors. Soon Julie and I, and perhaps Matthew, would enter the room with our arms full of boxes of Christmas decorations, and we would trim the tree and hang the garlands and place the wreaths in the windows and on the doors.

By this time my eyes would be filled with tears, and I'd resolve to keep my thoughts on safer ground. I honestly would try, but soon I'd be seeing the red-bowed wrappings on the gifts stacked beneath the tree. I could see myself sitting at the table in our elegant dining room, head bowed while Father said the grace. Then as he carved the turkey we would chat and laugh, just for the joy of being alive and together.

Wiping my eyes on the corner of my apron when no one was looking, I tried to gather my thoughts back to safer ground. And then I would find myself thinking of Jon and Mary and their family in Calgary. They, too, would be preparing for Christmas. I could see the house. I knew where every candle and holly wreath would be placed. I could see the children, their faces shining as they sat before the open fire listening to the familiar yet ever-new Christmas story. How I longed to be with them!

I wept. I prayed. I struggled. I felt I would never make it through this Christmas. Never in all of my life had I been so homesick.

Just hang on, I kept telling myself; *just keep yourself in hand. Soon it will be over and then you'll be all right again.* But I was beginning to wonder, to fear lest I would lose complete control, or at least make a scene. I did not want to give Wynn reason to be concerned about me. I tried even harder.

On December twenty-four we had class as usual. At noon I dismissed the children and tried to find something constructive to fill my afternoon. I didn't have the ingredients for special baking, nor gifts to wrap in pretty Christmasy tissue paper. Mostly I puttered around in the kitchen, feeling alone and empty.

Soon it would be time for Wynn to be coming home. It would officially be Christmas Eve. I stiffened my upper lip, breathed a little prayer and hoped to be able to stay in control. One eye watched the clock, while the other watched the stew I was stirring. My ears were waiting for the sound of approaching feet.

It was then that I heard running. I knew it was not Wynn. Wynn did not approach our house at a run. Kip knew it too. He was up and over to the door before I could even turn from the stove.

The door burst open and Susie, breathless and without outdoor wraps, flung herself into the room.

"Teacher," she gasped, "Teacher, come quick! Mama needs you."

I did not wait to ask why I was needed. I grabbed my parka, flung it about me and headed for the door. I stopped only long enough to hastily tie on my snowshoes, and then I followed the running Susie. I did think briefly that I had not even stopped to push the stew to the back of the stove.

When we reached the cabin, we were both out of breath. Susie pushed open the door and after throwing aside my snowshoes I followed her in. One dim lamp was burning and the thick smoke of the open fire stung my eyes so I could hardly see. As soon as my eyes adjusted, I could see that Susie's mother was not alone. A midwife was there. I then noticed the same unusual smell I had found at Nimmie's after her baby was born.

Susie's mother moaned and tossed on her bed. The Indian midwife moved closer to her and spoke words of comfort in a sing-songy voice. Neither woman seemed to have noticed me.

"What's the matter?" I whispered to Susie.

"The baby is already here, and still she pains—bad," explained Susie in a worried tone.

"The baby?"

"Yes. There."

Susie pointed to one corner of the room. A pile of furs was lying there and, as I looked closely, I felt more than saw something stir. I looked back to Susie. Fear showed in her eyes. I reached an arm out to her and pulled her close. She did not resist me. As I held the little girl, I wondered which one of us needed the consolation, the closeness, the most. My tears nearly spilled again.

The old midwife turned to get some more of her medicine. It was the first she seemed to be aware of us. She did not look surprised.

"Not good," she said in a low voice. "Not good. Pain should go now."

I was frightened. I knew Susie felt I should be able to do something. What could I do? I knew nothing about caring for birthing mothers. Surely we wouldn't have another family of children left as orphans? Susie had already lost her father six months before in a river accident. I prayed that she wouldn't be asked to give up her mother, too.

As I looked at the frail child in my arms and thought of what the future could hold for her, my concern over myself and my homesickness suddenly left me. All my thoughts were now on this family, this mother who tossed and groaned before us. What could we do? I began to pray for the mother.

A faint whimper from the corner interrupted my talk with God. The baby was awake. With one arm still around Susie, I moved toward the corner. The little one was small, with thick black hair framing the tiny face. I reached down to lift him up. As I cuddled him close, the whimpering stopped, but Susie, who still stood close to me, had not stopped shaking.

"We need to find Mr. Delaney," I told her. "He might have gone home by now, or he might be at the store. Do you think you can find him?"

She nodded her head.

"Put on your parka and your mittens this time," I said. "It's cold out and you mustn't get chilled. I'll be here with your mother."

She followed my instructions, bundled up and then left. I was sure she was running again.

We did not wait too long before Susie was back with Wynn. He didn't stop to ask questions but went over to the Indian woman on the corner bed and began to examine her. I still clung to the baby. The little warm body in my arms seemed to give me some measure of assurance.

"Maggie," I heard Wynn speak to the Indian lady, "Maggie, do you hear me?"

The woman only groaned.

"She sleep now," said the midwife. "Get rest."

"Not get rest, yet," said Wynn. "She still has a big job left. She has a baby to deliver."

"Baby come already," the midwife informed Wynn and pointed at the baby I held in my arms.

"Maybe so," said Wynn, "but now it is time for the brother to come."

Twins! I couldn't believe it. I guess Susie couldn't either.

"What does he mean, Teacher?" she asked in a whisper.

"Your mother is going to have two babies—twins," I said to her.

"Like bear cubs?" she whispered, her eyes big.

I laughed softly.

"Like bear cubs," I told her.

By the time the second baby arrived, and the new babies and the tired mother were properly taken care of, it was no longer Christmas Eve. Wynn and I walked home arm-in-arm over the crunching snow, our breath sending little puffs before us in the cold, crisp night air. The moon shone overhead, and the northern lights played back and forth across the heavens. I wondered aloud about that night long ago, when another child was born on Christmas Eve. It always seemed like a miracle when a new life entered the world, and tonight there had been two new lives and they both seemed well and healthy. Wynn had been wrong, though; it was not a brother. The second baby, much to Susie's delight, had been a girl.

Chapter Sixteen

Winter Visitor

Christmas Day was still a time of loneliness for me, but
I did not feel overwhelmed with homesickness. Wynn and I
spent the day before our fire. Our dinner was venison roast
and vegetables, with a blueberry pie for dessert. We had
planned to go for a walk along the river but the day turned
out to be too cold for that.

We did exchange gifts. We didn't have much, but each of
us had hidden away a few items for future giving when we
had come north. With two Christmases, our anniversary and
Wynn's birthday behind us, I was now at the end of my little
horde. I wondered what I would do for a gift when Wynn's
birthday came around again. The question nibbled at the
back of my mind while I watched him unwrap the new knife
which was this year's present. Perhaps I could find something to purchase from one of the Indian ladies.

My gift from Wynn brought a gasp of joy. It was two pairs
of new stockings. I had mended and repaired the ones I owned
numerous times, and I did so hate mended stockings. I found
out later that Wynn had ordered them in from Edmonton
through Ian's store with the fall supply train.

The day seemed to be rather long. There wasn't much to
do except talk. We had few games to play, no music available,

and the miserable weather left us no chance to leave the cabin.

While I prepared an evening snack of cold meat sandwiches and leftover pie, Wynn stretched out on the rug before the fire. By the time I returned to join him, he had fallen asleep. I knew my sleeping husband was tired. His job took so much of his time and energy. After delivering the baby last night, he had been called from our overcooked stew to see a sick child.

He had lost weight, too. I hadn't noticed it until now, but he definitely did not weigh as much as he had when we came north. I looked down at my own body. I had lost a few pounds, too, which was reasonable. We were active, walked a lot, and ate few foods that would add pounds to our frames.

I looked at my hands. They were no longer the soft hands of a pampered woman. Time had changed us—time and the northland.

I didn't know whether to waken Wynn or to let him sleep, so I just sat watching him, undecided.

Suddenly Kip arose and looked toward the door, his head cocked to one side as he listened. Was someone coming?

"No, God, please," I pleaded. "Don't let Wynn be needed again tonight."

By the time I heard the footsteps, Kip was already at the door. I could tell by his bark that whoever was coming was not someone he knew. Kip welcomed most of the settlement people with only a wagging of his tail.

Kip's barking awakened Wynn and he pushed himself up into a sitting position and looked apologetically at me.

"Sorry. I must have—" but he got no further.

There was stamping at our front door and then someone was banging on it.

Kip's barking increased, and Wynn rose to his feet and motioned him to go to his corner in silence; Kip obeyed rather reluctantly, I thought.

Wynn opened the door and a man almost fell into the room. The first thing I noticed was his clothes. He was dressed in the uniform of the Royal North West Mounted Police.

Then I noticed that he had a big bundle in his arms. He looked out from around it and his face, red with the cold of the bitter wind, broke into a sort of frozen smile.

"Sergeant Wynn Delaney?" he asked.

"Right," said Wynn and moved to relieve him of his heavy load so he would have a free hand to shake in greeting. But the man laughed softly and moved the parcel away from Wynn's outstretched hand.

"Sorry," he said, "but I have strict orders to hand this over to Elizabeth Delaney and no one else." He turned to me. "You're Mrs. Elizabeth Delaney?"

My mouth must have dropped open in astonishment. "I— I am," I stammered.

He handed me the parcel as if he was awfully glad to be rid of it. Then he brushed the snow from his parka, pulled off his mitten and reached out a hand to Wynn.

"Carl Havens of the Royal North West Mounted Police," he said evenly.

I stood with the parcel in my hands, looking wide-eyed at the young officer. How had he gotten to our small cabin in the North? What was he doing here? And where was this strange box from? Wynn was speaking, "Welcome to the North, Carl. Won't you take off your coat and tell us what this is all about? I believe Elizabeth has just brewed a fresh pot of coffee."

So it was over that fresh pot of coffee in front of our fireplace that Carl Havens filled us in on what he was doing in our area and how he happened to be our Christmas visitor.

He had been stationed in Calgary and had come to know our Julie through the small church there. When he received his new posting, and it was up North, Julie expressed a desire to send a Christmas package to her northern family. Havens checked with the Force and they gave their permission for him to act as courier. And so here was Officer Havens on his way to his posting, which was north and a little east of ours, stopping by to see us with a parcel of goodies from home!

It seemed too good to be true.

The little gifts from Jon and Mary, each of the children, and Julie in particular, should have brightened my Christmas. And I guess it did. It also made me even lonelier. I cried over everything I lifted from its wrappings. The men seemed to understand, and no one tried to talk me out of my tears.

I fixed more sandwiches. Officer Havens was famished, as though he had not eaten for days. I thought of the misery of the trail. It was hard enough traveling it in the warmth of summer. It must be nearly unbearable in the winter's cold. I wondered how the young Mountie had ever found his way to us in the snow.

"I'm traveling with guides," he said in answer to our questions. "They are camped down by the trading post. We will spend the night there and then go on in the morning. The man at the store—McLain, is it?—told me where to find you, and of course I couldn't rest until I got that parcel delivered—and right on time, too."

He smiled as I wondered just how serious the relationship was between him and Julie. He seemed like a fine young man. He'd be good for Julie.

As we had our coffee and sandwiches I plied him with questions about the family and life in Calgary. Like a fresh breath of home, it was so good to get some news of the outside world.

It was late when he said he must go. His men would be wondering where he was. They had to leave early in the morning.

Wynn invited him back for breakfast the next morning, but he declined. He would eat with his men, he said. Wynn promised to see him before he left, and then he was gone through the snow, just as he had come.

I had a strange feeling as I watched his tall figure depart into the darkness.

"Wynn," I asked, "was he really here, or have I been dreaming?"

Wynn pointed to the gifts now scattered around our small cabin.

"It looks like he was really here, Beth."

It had been a long time since Wynn had used my pet name. I blinked back tears, not sure if they were tears of joy or sorrow. I still missed my family. The gifts were nice, but they did not take the place of the ones who had sent them. I also loved my husband dearly. Yes, my choice was the same. *As long as Wynn is in the North, I will be here with him.*

He took me gently in his arms and kissed away the tear that lay on my cheek.

"It's been tough this Christmas, hasn't it?"

I nodded.

"I'm sorry you've been so lonesome," he went on.

"You noticed?"

"I noticed."

"I thought I was hiding it pretty well."

He hugged me closer. "I appreciate your trying, Beth, though I would have been more than happy to share it, to talk about it. It might have helped a bit. Sometimes I get lonesome, too. I think about home, about Mother—about the fact that I wasn't there when Dad passed away. I wish I would have been. I worry some that the same thing might happen with Mother. Every day I pray, 'Please, God, let me be there this time.' Does that sound foolish? I mean, can you understand?"

"I understand," I said as my arms tightened around him. I did understand. Wynn had family, too, that he loved deeply. It wasn't easy for him to serve in the North. But the people here needed him. It was his commitment to them that kept him with the Force, that kept him here in the small settlement. I had seen the same light of commitment in the eyes of the other young Mountie, Carl Havens. He, too, felt that being a member of the Royal North West Mounted Police was more than a job. It was a calling to serve people. Wynn's even higher calling to serve his Lord was fulfilled in his responsibilities here among the trappers and Indians.

I reached up to kiss my husband, and with the kiss was a promise—a promise of my love and support here by his side for as long as he felt that the North needed him.

Chapter Seventeen

Classes Resume

Jim Buck appeared at my door the next morning. I had not expected to start classes again for another day or two, but Jim either did not understand or pretended not to.

"Come for school," he said in answer to my puzzled look.

I did not turn him away. He came in and took his place at the table, and I brought him a few books to look at while I finished my morning tasks.

He buried himself in the books and paid no attention to me.

"What about Susie?" I asked him. "If we are having class again, shouldn't she be here, and Wawasee?"

"They come—maybe," said Jim, afraid I might change my mind.

"But they don't know about it," I continued.

"You bang bell," responded Jim, solving that dilemma.

I smiled to myself and went to "bang bell."

After a few moments Wawasee appeared. Tucked in his parka was his beloved scribbler. He proudly showed it to me, every page filled with his drawings. They were very well done, and I marveled that a child of his age, with no training or guidance, could accomplish such beautiful and skilled artwork.

I settled him at the table and assigned him to draw the

illustrations on some more word cards. Then I listened to Jim's reading lesson. He was doing well.

The morning passed and Susie did not appear. I was concerned about her, and after the two boys had gone home and I had eaten my lunch and cleared the table, I decided to go over to Susie's cabin and see how things were going.

Susie's mother, Maggie, still lay on the bed in the corner along with her twins. They both looked fine, though one cried vigorously while the other slept through it all.

There was much commotion and confusion in the cabin. An elderly couple was moving in. The woman was going to care for Maggie and the babies, and as the old man also needed her care, she had brought him with her.

Susie had been sent to gather some firewood to keep the fire burning. I thought of the wood supply beside the cabin we used as our schoolhouse. Once we had stopped having classes in the schoolroom, the people of the village had taken advantage of the wood supply and helped themselves. I supposed there would be little left by now.

With two more people moving into the cabin, I wondered where they would sleep. It was already crowded with the family which presently occupied it. Besides Susie, Maggie had two small boys and now there were also the new twins.

I went over to the bedside to talk to Maggie. She still seemed weak. She smiled at me though and nodded her head at each baby. "Two," she said to me. I smiled in return.

"How are you, Maggie?" I asked her.

"Not good," she said, shaking her head; then her face brightened. "But soon."

"I'll have the sergeant drop by to see you. He might have some medicine to make you strong faster," I promised, wondering even as I said it if Wynn had any kind of tonic or vitamins.

"That good," she said. She lay for a minute and then went on, "Susie hear bell. Want to go. I need today. Now Too Many come. But Susie might go stay with other family in big village. No room here."

Maggie's face looked sorrowful at the thought.

"What do you mean?" I asked, horrified at what I thought she meant.

"No room," Maggie repeated.

I looked about me. She was right. There was no room to put another bed on the floor, yet somehow, two more would need to be squeezed in.

Without even stopping to think or to draw a breath, I said, "I have room. I'll keep her at my house; then she won't need to go to the big village, and she will be able to come and see you and help gather your wood, and—"

"That is good," agreed Maggie. "You take."

I could hardly wait for Susie to return from her wood gathering so I could tell her the good news. *She was coming to stay with me; she could continue with her classes,* I rejoiced. She would not need to leave her village or her people.

Susie received the news with quiet joy. Except for the shine in her eyes, I would not have thought she heard me.

She did not tell her mother goodbye, but I noticed their eyes exchange a glance, and I knew that both mother and daughter felt the parting. Susie would be near, so she would be able to return home each day to help in the household tasks and to visit her mother.

We started for our cabin, Susie carrying all she owned in a tiny bundle. I wondered how anyone, even a small girl, could survive with so few belongings.

As we walked silently across the clearing, the sun shone brightly from a cloudless sky, the kind of a day that lends itself to snow blindness because of the intense glare of the winter snow. I saw Susie squinting against it, and I supposed I squinted, too.

Won't Wynn be surprised when he comes home tonight, I thought. There was not a doubt in my mind but what Wynn would heartily approve of my actions. I was sure he would take in the whole village if he felt it would be for their good.

Kip welcomed Susie with generous wags of his tail. Perhaps he had missed her at class today. She placed her small bundle on the floor and threw her arms around his neck.

"I am going to live with you, Silver One," she said, calling him by his Indian name.

Kip seemed to like the arrangement. His whole body waved with his enthusiasm.

It was then I noticed a little skipping of my heart. *The cabin won't seem so empty now when Wynn is away.* It would be filled with the voice of a child.

Chapter Eighteen

Susie

It did make a difference to have Susie in our home. Where it had been quiet and empty before, it now became filled with laughter and childish games. Susie was a bright little thing who loved to chatter and laugh. Kip was her playmate. They romped together on the rug and furniture, and sometimes I was tempted to admonish them to be quiet and still. Then I would think of the house as it used to be, and how it would be again when Susie left us, and I would hold back the command.

Susie's grasp of English broadened quickly. She loved my books. When I was busy she would pore over them, trying to sound out the words. When I was free she would ask me to read to her, which didn't take too much coaxing because I loved it as much as she did.

I was careful to send her home for a portion of each day. While she was gone I worked quickly at whatever needed to be done so that when she returned I would be free to spend my time with her.

Some days I dressed warmly and went with her to the woods to help her gather the wood supply for her cabin. We always took Kip along, and he loved the romp through the snow. It was good for all of us, and we returned home with rosy cheeks and shining eyes, delighted by the things we had seen in the forest.

We didn't neglect Susie's schoolwork. In fact, I guess we advanced it. We both loved the excitement of learning. Susie shared with me many things about her people, and I told her many things about mine. She was a real help to me in understanding the ways of the Indians, and I had a wonderful chance to learn more of their language.

Though Susie would laugh at my attempts to pronounce some of the strange words, she was a good little teacher and would have me repeat the word over and over until I got it right. In my heart I hoped for the day when she would be standing in front of a classroom, teaching her own people. I was sure now that Wynn and Nimmie were right. One or two of these dear children could open the door to a new world for the entire tribe. Perhaps Susie, with her quick mind and love for laughter, would be the key to that door.

Wynn loved Susie too. At first she was shy around him. She respected the lawman, and perhaps even liked him, but she held back, a gentle smile showing only in her dark eyes.

Kip was certainly not shy. Whenever Wynn returned home, Kip met him at the door with joyous yips and wagging tail. Wynn was hardly allowed to remove his heavy winter wraps before Kip expected a tussle. Wynn would take the big, silver-tipped, furry head between his hands and press his face against the dog's fluffy coat. Then the two of them would rock back and forth, and often end up rolling on the floor.

Susie watched it all at first, her eyes round with astonishment. I'm sure she had never seen such goings-on before, not with a grown-up. Occasionally Kip would look her direction and whimper, as if inviting her to join them. Then Susie would turn away and come to me to see if I had some task I might wish her to do.

After Kip had been satisfied, Wynn would come to me. At first we weren't sure how we should conduct ourselves in Susie's presence. We felt she was probably not used to seeing an embrace and welcoming kiss among adults in the way we were accustomed. Should we, for Susie's sake, restrain ourselves? We tried that for one day. But we missed it so, we decided that Susie probably could adjust to our way of showing affection. So when Wynn came to the stove to see what was cooking, we embraced and greeted one another with a kiss just as we always had done.

At first we noticed Susie's big black eyes upon us, but as the days went by she seemed to accept it as part of the strange rituals of our household.

Wynn never failed to turn to the little girl with a question about her day. At first she was shy and hesitant, but gradually she became more open. They even shared Indian words I did not yet know. He would ask her a question in her own language and she would answer him, a twinkle in her eyes. This exchange was often followed with laughter, and I took pleasure in their private little jokes.

Susie was quick to observe. When Wynn came in and removed his winter things, he also took off his heavy boots and put on lighter, more comfortable footwear. He sat in the one big chair before the fire to remove the boots. Then he walked, stocking-footed, to our bedroom to get his slippers. Each night his little ritual was the same. Until one evening when Susie changed it.

Wynn had lowered his tired body into his chair and was tugging at the heavy boots. He sat for a moment relaxing the strained muscles, and then rose to go to the bedroom, but there was Susie, standing in front of him, his slippers in her outstretched hand.

Wynn's eyes first showed surprise, and then he beamed at her. He reached out—not for the boots but for the little girl. He pulled her to him and hugged her close. Susie did not pull back.

I wondered as I watched if this was the first time Susie had been hugged by a man. Her own father would have been a very busy trapper, often gone from the home and not accustomed to showing his love in this way, though no one could doubt that Indian fathers did love their children. Often they were seen talking and playing with them, their eyes aglow with pride and joy. I often thought as I watched, that had they been called upon to do so, I'm sure they would have given their lives for their children without a moment's hesitation.

But here was little Susie getting a warm hug. Would she understand it?

"Thank you, my girl," Wynn was saying. And then he said a few words in the Indian dialect and Susie giggled. Wynn released her and put on his slippers. Susie's eyes never left his face.

"Seeing as I didn't have to walk *all* the way to the bedroom to get my slippers, there might be time for a short story before Elizabeth calls us for supper," Wynn said with a nod toward the small stack of books.

Susie's smile grew broader and she ran for her favorite. I inobtrusively postponed supper a little. Wynn lifted Susie up onto his knee and soon both of them were completely absorbed in the story. As I watched them, tears brimmed in my eyes. This was as it should be. This was what I wanted to give to Wynn—a child, a child of his own to love and care for and cuddle. Instinctively I had known Wynn would make a good father. I had been right. I could see it clearly now in the way that he held Susie.

We were a real family now. Wynn, me and Susie. There was a family feeling in our small cabin. We had been happy together, Wynn and I, but a child was what we needed to make our life complete.

I looked at Wynn and the little girl on his knee. Their eyes were riveted to the pages of the storybook. My heart sang a little song. I loved Susie so much and I knew with certainty that she loved me in return. It was such fun to romp through the snow, to make cookies, to teach her how to embroider, to help her to make the rag doll, to . . . There were so many things we had done together in the short time since Susie had come to us. I thought ahead to all the things I still wanted to share with her.

And then a flash of insight shocked me back to reality.

I faced the fact that Susie would not be with us long. I would love to keep her. I knew Wynn would love to keep her. My heart ached as I formed the words, *But she is not truly ours*, though my mind cried out against the fact. She belonged to another family. I knew this would not change, nor would I change it if I could. Susie loved her family. Her family loved her. Ultimately she belonged with them.

I must daily remind myself of that and do nothing that would make it any harder for Susie when she returned to her own home. My deep love must protect her *from* my love. It seemed like a strange enigma, but I knew that it was true. It would be so easy to pretend Susie was mine. To take over her life. To try to make her white instead of Indian.

We would love her. We both would love her. But we—and especially I—must be conscious of who she was and preserve and keep that for her, at the same time expanding her world. It would not be easy, but I would try with all my heart.

Susie will eventually go home, I must always remember that. Perhaps by that time I would be expecting our own child. Susie would be deeply missed, but it would help to know that someone, some other little one, was on the way to fill the emptiness.

I waited for the story to end and then called them both for supper. We bowed our heads for the evening grace and Susie reached out for a hand from each of us, our custom when praying together.

I held the little hand in mine and said my own quiet prayer as Wynn prayed aloud. I prayed for Susie, our dear little girl. I would always think of her as ours. Uniquely ours. And yet not. I prayed that God would give me daily wisdom. I prayed for her salvation. I prayed for the salvation of her mother and family. Without that, Susie did not have much chance when she went back home.

My thinking changed as I sat there bowed in prayer. I

saw clearly that if I wanted to affect Susie's life for good, then I had to work with her whole family. I must do more. I must reach out. I needed God's help and direction.

Wynn and I had a long talk that night after Susie went to bed. I told him how God had been speaking to me, and he held me close as I talked. I was right, he assured me. Susie's world was not our world. We had to prepare her for a return to her own, whenever that time would be.

Our days changed, though outwardly our household routine stayed the same. Susie and I spent our time together. I always went with her to gather the wood and take it to her house. While we chatted I tried to learn much more about her people. When we went to her house I spent more time talking with her mother and the little boys. I dared to try the words Susie had been teaching me. Sometimes they did not come out right and Susie would giggle, but she would correct me, and I would go on.

I even spoke to the elderly couple, often sharing bits and pieces of my faith with them. I wanted them to understand, to come to know God. They listened politely but they did not yet question me further as I hoped and prayed they would.

At the end of the day when Wynn returned home, often weary from the day's heavy demands, Kip would always meet him at the door; but now Susie was usually there too. Sometimes she jumped right in and got in on the roll on the floor. Then as Wynn took off his heavy boots, she would run to the bedroom for his slippers.

I made sure supper was not so rushed that there wasn't time for the short story from a book, as Wynn and Susie cuddled in the big chair and he read to her. As much as she loved me, I felt that this was probably her favorite time of day.

We said our table grace in her Indian language. We wanted Susie to feel it was not "the white man's God" we prayed to. He could be her God as well. And when we knelt together beside the small cot for her bedtime prayer at the end of the day, we again prayed in words Susie had learned in her cradle.

We were building together now, though Susie might have been unaware of it. We held her and loved her, cuddled and guided her, but all the time we did so it was with a consciousness that we were preparing her, and ourselves, for that inevitable day when our paths would separate and we would again walk down different trails.

Chapter Nineteen

Spring Returns

Because of Susie, our days were more than filled with good things to do. I still taught class, the two village boys joining Susie each morning.

Susie was now far more outgoing and talkative than most of the settlement children. I wondered if she would find it hard to fit in with the other children again, and feared a bit for her. For this reason I began to suggest that she take some time each day to share in the village games.

She did not hesitate. She went gladly and from my observations seemed to have no difficulty at all in getting back in with her friends.

One day I had sent Susie out to play and then decided to walk to the store for a few items I needed. That would give me time to have tea with Nimmie. We still had our weekly Bible studies together, and Susie always joined us, her eyes big with wonder at the things we read and discussed. She had already decided she wanted to give her heart to this Jesus who loved her enough to die for her; and together Nimmie and I explained the gospel and what it meant to follow Him. She was such a precious child, with such a simple faith.

But now I was looking forward to just talking of women's things with Nimmie. She was already showing her pregnancy. Her two babies would not be too far apart in age.

Funny, I thought, *here is Nimmie, married for many years without children, and now she will be a mother twice, in such a short period of time.* I smiled to myself. Perhaps that's what God had in store for me. But I did hope that I didn't have to wait as long as Nimmie had waited.

I drew near a cluster of children deeply absorbed in their play. They did not even turn to look at me as I walked by. They were seated on the snow, their eyes turned eastward, their faces intent. And then I spotted Susie. She was at the front of the group, holding up some old cue cards I had given her. She was the teacher, and they were the pupils. I stood still in astonishment. I could not believe my eyes.

"What's this one?" I heard her clear voice ask.

Many hands went up eagerly. Susie pointed to a small girl.

"Fish," said the child.

"Right," said Susie, beaming her approval. "It's *fish*."

I shook my head to clear it. How come they would not attend my school, yet here they were? Then I began to laugh softly. Hadn't Nimmie said so all the time? *Teach one, they will teach others.* Here was Susie, in play, doing something I had been unable to do.

I must be sure she has more cards, I told myself and then hurried on to Nimmie's. I could hardly wait to share this exciting news with her.

I had not done my usual chaffing and fussing about the coming of spring, and so it was rather a surprise to me when Wynn remarked one night, "I expect the ice to break in the river soon. The Indian men are expecting it to be quite a spectacle this year because of the deep freezing. They say you can watch it all from that high bluff east of the settlement. Are you interested?"

I looked at Wynn in astonishment, suddenly realizing that there truly was very little snow left around the village and that the Indian women were again out searching the nearby meadows for new growth for the cooking pots. I really had not given it much thought, my days and hours having been so taken with other things.

Susie was already jumping up and down, clapping her little hands together.

"Of course," I answered. "But why this year? Why is it any different this time?" I wondered.

"We've had colder weather. The river is frozen deeper than usual. Some of the men even fear for the fish in some areas where the water is not too deep."

I hadn't even realized that the weather had been colder than usual.

"The warm weather has come more quickly," went on Wynn. "Haven't you noticed how quickly the snow disappeared? There may be flood problems this year."

I stopped on my way to the stove, a pot in my hand. My eyes widened.

"Are we in—" I checked myself and glanced toward Susie. She was listening to every word. Wynn picked up my thought.

"There will be no danger for our village. We are high enough on the crest of this bluff, but some of the villages farther downstream might have difficulty."

I still hadn't made it to the stove with the cooking pot. "What can be done?" I asked Wynn.

"Ian and I and a couple of other men are going out tomorrow to look things over. We may ask some of them to move their belongings up onto higher ground. I hope they won't resist this. A few of the older ones might remember when the river flooded before, about twenty-six years ago. It nearly wiped out a village at that time. Those who remember might be willing to move and lead the way for the others."

Then Wynn abruptly changed his tone and the topic.

"Let's not borrow trouble," he stated philosophically. "Susie, would you like to see the ice go out of the river?"

She answered him with an Indian word, one filled with meaning of joy and anticipation. He laughed and tousled her black hair.

"Then that settles it," he said. "We'll go."

"When? When?" Susie jumped up and down in excitement.

"I'm not sure—just yet. Two men are watching the river. They will let us know when it is about to happen."

"How can they tell?" Susie echoed my own unasked question. Wynn laughed.

"Well, I'm not too sure just how they tell. All I know is that they seem to know every time. They watch carefully for certain signs. They listen to the sound of the river and the ice. They know."

"And they will tell us?" Susie wanted lots of assurance.

Wynn nodded his head.

"In time?" persisted Susie. "In time for us to get to the hill?"

Wynn smiled at her impatience.

"In plenty of time," he assured her.

I continued to the stove with my pot and put it on, almost subconsciously passing a hand over the big iron firebox to test out its hottest spot. I then put in more wood and turned back to Wynn.

"I guess I was just expecting some more snowstorms," I confessed. "I hadn't really allowed myself to hope 'spring' yet."

"I'm not saying that we won't get another snow or two," he cautioned, "but if it comes it shouldn't last long. I think spring is here to stay."

I turned to set the table and realized Susie had already put on the plates, the cups and the cutlery.

I reached a hand to her shoulder to thank her.

"Susie," I said, "how would you like to learn how to plant your own garden?"

She turned shining eyes to me. "Oh, yes!" she exclaimed. "Like Mrs. Ian?"

"Mrs. Ian" was the children's name for Nimmie.

"Like Mrs. Ian," I replied.

"She lets us taste her things sometimes," added Susie. "If we promise not to steal when she's not looking."

Yes, Nimmie would call the act exactly what it was. No soft-pedalling it by giving it some lesser name.

"Indians don't steal," went on Susie seriously, " 'cause we share everything. But to be polite we should ask. And if they are not looking and we take, and hide, that means to steal."

"That's right," I agreed rather absently.

"An' white folks don't like stealers," continued Susie. She cast a furtive glance at Wynn. "They lock people up."

I knew she was identifying Wynn as the one who would do the "locking."

Wynn looked up from pulling off his boots.

"We don't lock up children," he said rather firmly.

"You don't?" Was it relief or doubt in Susie's voice?

"No, we don't," said Wynn defensively.

I knew he was often irritated at being used as the boogeyman with so many children.

Susie stood quietly for a moment and then a twinkle entered her black eyes.

"Wait 'til I tell the rest," she said. "We can do anything we want—"

But Wynn did not let her finish. Realizing even before I did that Susie was teasing him, he threw aside his heavy boot and with one off, one on, he was off after the young child. Susie ran shrieking, laughter making it hard for her to get away. There really wasn't much room to run in our little cabin anyway, so after one trip around the table Wynn had caught her. Kip could not resist becoming involved in the tussle. I stood in my little spot in front of the stove, watching all the commotion and hoping the wild howls and barking would not carry all the way to the settlement. Our neighbors would wonder what in the world was going on.

"That's enough," I finally said, and motioned Kip to his corner.

"We'd better stop," Wynn joked with Susie, "before Elizabeth sends us to a corner, too."

Susie was panting lightly from the exertion. For a few

minutes she was quiet as Wynn helped her up and deposited her on the cot.

Then she turned to him, her eyes big and questioning. "It's not true, then, is it? You don't lock children away so they never see their folks again?"

"You are right, Susie. We never lock children away."

"Then what do you do if they be bad?"

"We talk to the mothers and fathers and try to get them to help their children be good. We talk to the children and tell them all the dangers of continuing to be bad. We don't want children to grow up to be bad people. It makes everyone very sad. We don't like to lock up people—not anyone. But sometimes we have to keep grown-ups who insist on being bad from hurting other people."

Susie thought about this.

She nodded her little dark head, very serious now. "You're like Jesus," she said thoughtfully.

Wynn's eyes widened. "Pardon me?"

"You're like Jesus," Susie said, more positively now that she had said the words out loud. "He doesn't like it when people be bad either. An' He doesn't like to send them away— out of heaven. But it would spoil heaven for everybody else if He let bad people in there."

Wynn said nothing, but his eyes looked misty as he reached out to tousle the little black head on his way to the bedroom for his slippers.

It was a clear, sunny day, and I had to admit as I took deep breaths of air that spring really was with us again. I eagerly looked forward to all the promises of another growing season. I loved the summer months in this beautiful land—if only there was some way to bypass the hordes of mosquitoes and blackflies. But even with them to torment me, I would cherish the summer months ahead.

The children played and the adults chatted on the bluff east of the village while we waited for the spectacular sight of the river breaking up. Ian and Wynn and the two men whom they took with them had already found that two villages would be in danger in case of flooding. They had talked with the people and urged them to leave their log cabins and move their belongings to higher ground. Some of the people had listened. Others insisted they were high enough to escape any rampaging river waters. Wynn had argued and explained as best he could, but a few had remained adamant. Finally Wynn had left them, after a promise that they would keep a man on guard to watch the river.

So now we waited on the brow of the hill, watching to see what would happen when the river threw off the heavy garments of winter and flung itself free from the icy restraints.

I smiled to myself. I felt all of us were just using this as an excuse to get away from the village and have a party on the hill. Some of us had even prepared picnic lunches for the occasion.

There was a happy hum all about me as people visited with one another. The shouts of the children rang out on the quiet of the day. They were thoroughly enjoying the outing.

It shows how short we are on entertainment, I said to myself, *when we will all walk two miles to a hill to watch river ice break up.*

And then there was a strange, eery hush. All heads turned toward the river, leaving sentences unfinished, hanging forgotten on the morning air.

I would never have believed that our quiet, placid river could react with such a wild, untamed frenzy, but as we watched she lifted her head with a defiance that both surprised and frightened me.

A low moan quickly turned into a thunderous roar, and then there was a cracking that shattered the air with its intensity. As the sound rent the stillness, huge blocks of ice were thrown many feet in the air and hurled forward. There was a shifting and grinding, and foam and angry waters began to whip the shores where the ice had been. I stared in silent amazement.

The waters and ice blocks rushed writhing and foaming

as though intent on some evil, roaring out vengeful messages.

The turbulent waters rushed on to a sharp bend in the river. There they seemed to stop, struggling and lashing like some dying giant. And then a shout went up, and another followed, and soon people were milling all about me, crying out to one another in anguished tones. I could understand none of it. My eyes turned back to the river. The ice blocks were piling higher and higher, and behind them was a tumbling, twisting sea of troubled water.

I looked around me for Wynn. Then for Susie.

I spotted Susie with Kip in a group of village children. Their eyes too were turned to the bend in the river. Even as I watched, the water slowly slipped up the banks of the river and spilled out on either side, still gray and angry looking.

I saw Wynn then. He raised his hand to command the attention of the people. Slowly the group became quiet again, only the distant roaring of the river and the grinding and crunching of the ice breaking the silence.

"Women and children stay here," Wynn was calling over the noise.

I looked wildly about. Nimmie was moving quietly toward me.

"What does he mean?" I asked her, puzzled and frightened.

"The river," she said. I thought I detected fear in her voice. "It has jammed at the bend."

I turned to the river and swung quickly back to Nimmie. I didn't have to ask my question.

"It did that one other year," Nimmie continued. "Everything in the village was lost."

"No," I almost screamed, my hands going to my face as I pictured our cozy home submerged under that icy flow.

Nimmie reached out a hand to me. It was then I realized that Susie was pressing her little body up against me. *Susie's mother is still in the cabin!* I thought wildly. She was not strong enough yet to make the pilgrimage to the bluff. With her were her twin babies, the boy and the girl, and the elderly couple who had been living with them.

My hands went down to pull Susie close. I forgot all about our cabin, Wynn's and mine, and the things in it that made it home to us. My concern was for Susie's family and the other people who might still remain in the village.

Men were running now, running toward the village. My eyes were huge as I realized that was a two-mile run. *How much time do they have?* And then I noticed that men were also running the other way—toward the jammed-up river.

"What—?" I began, and Nimmie answered, "They are going to try to break the jam."

"But how?" I stammered, and then I saw that Wynn was leading the runners toward the river.

"O God, no. Please, no," and I covered my face with my hands and sank down in a heap on the ground, pulling Susie down with me.

I began to shake uncontrollably. What could mere man do against the giant ice blocks? "O God. O God!" was all I could moan.

And then someone was patting my shoulder. I tried to pull myself together enough to respond. It was Susie. Her face too was white and her eyes wide with fear.

"We need to pray," she whispered. "We need to pray quick—before they get there. Before—" her chin was trembling. "I don't want another father killed by the ice," she continued, and I remembered hearing the story of how Susie's father had been dragged under the river's ice while trying to save his dog team and his winter's catch of furs so he could feed his family.

I pulled Susie to me. Sobs were shaking her now.

"Dear God," I implored desperately, "please, please turn them back!" Then more calmly, "Protect us, God. Protect each one of us. Protect the men who have gone to the river. Keep them safe, Lord. Be with Wynn. And be with the men who have gone to the village. May they get there in time to save the people. Amen."

I went to draw Susie to me, but she resisted. Instead, she began to pray in her own language. She implored the God who sent His Son Jesus, the same Jesus who made all things, to set free the river's waters so it would be able to continue on downstream and not be held back by the ice. She reminded God that Wynn would not lock children up—he just wanted to teach them not to be bad when they grew up, that was all. And then she told God that she loved Him, too, and would try her hardest, all her life, not to be bad, so that she'd never need to be locked up or sent away from heaven. She said "Amen" in English to close her prayer.

When Susie finished praying, I hated to open my eyes. Yet I had to see. Yes, there were the men still running down the long slope of the hill toward the river. The water was much higher and angrier now. It swirled and smashed and swung at the blocks of shifting ice. I was sure as I watched that they would never be able to do anything to free them. I prayed silently again that they would not try but would turn and run for safety before the river could sweep them away in its angry flood.

They were far enough away from us now that I could not pick out Wynn in the retreating figures. And then I saw an arm upraised and I knew it was Wynn's. He had gathered the men around and was giving them orders. It was the first I realized that many of the men were carrying their guns.

"They will fire rifle shots into the ice blocks," Nimmie was saying. And then she added, rather forlornly, I thought, "It has never worked, yet it's all there is to try."

They began to move on again. They were at the water's edge with the swirling waters all around them. As one, they lifted their rifles to their shoulders. There was deafening silence and then I heard Susie whisper, "Now, Jesus," and there was a sudden explosion. Ice flew hundreds of feet in the air, spewing out in every direction. For a few moments all was silent, and then a mighty cheer went up. The river was flowing again. It was still flooding the land beneath us, it was still raging and roaring, but there was movement downstream now. The river was free to move on.

I pulled Susie to me. She didn't appear to be one bit surprised. I held her close and rocked her back and forth, the tears, unheeded, pouring down my face.

"He did it, Susie!" I cried. "He did it."

People were beginning to move toward the village, many excited voices floating back to us on the breeze.

I stood up on shaky legs, drawing Susie up also.

"Come on, Susie," I said, hugging her to me, "let's go home now. Our village is safe. Let's go meet Wynn and we'll all go home together."

But Susie held back.

"What's the matter?" I asked her.

"You said," began Susie slowly, "you said we're s'posed to say thank you to Him."

Susie was so right, and so we did.

Chapter Twenty

Changes

As Wynn had feared, the two down-river villages were flooded by the spring river waters. But because of the precautions taken in moving the people to higher ground, no lives and little property were lost. I think we all breathed easier when the flood waters finally receded and the river returned to its normal peaceful self.

As spring turned into summer, Susie's mother gained strength. She was now able to be outside at times, simply sitting in the sun. The twins were growing and becoming roly-poly and merry. Susie loved to play with them and often had one or the other in her arms or on her back. She continued to live with us, for her family's cabin was still crowded. The elderly woman, Too Many, remained to care for Maggie and the children.

Susie and I planted our garden and took great pleasure in watching the tender plants put forth their first two green leaves and then expand and grow as they drank in the summer sun. We pulled weeds and carried water when we felt that nature had not sent enough rain. The garden grew, and Susie asked nearly every day when we would have our first vegetables.

Nimmie's new baby was a healthy boy, and Ian's fatherly

pride was felt all around the village. Nimmie looked pleased, too.

"Now I have both an herb-gatherer and a hunter," she told me, happiness making her face glow.

I suppose I envied Nimmie. I would have felt it even more if it had not been for Susie and the way she helped to fill my days.

I still visited her mother, Maggie, as often as I dared without making myself a real nuisance. I took her little things, chatted with her about her family, shared Susie's and my experiences, helped carry wood and water, but mostly I watched for every chance I had to tell her a little more about God and His love for her. Little by little I noticed sparks of interest in her.

Nimmie promised to help me. We prayed together for Susie's family; and Nimmie, too, made frequent calls, offering help and sharing little experiences about how God was with her each day. Nimmie watched for opportunities to assure Maggie that God was not only interested in the affairs of the white man, but that He loved Indian people, too.

We dismissed school classes the middle of June. The children were much too busy in the summer months to have time for study. I really was much too busy also. Wawasee still brought his drawings to show me and begged, with his eyes only, for another scribbler whenever he had filled the one he was working in.

Jim Buck did not come. He was being teased and bullied by the older boys in the settlement about his interest in school. I ached for Jim. He had a sharp mind that should be educated, but what would happen when school resumed? Would he be able to take the taunting and teasing of the others for the sake of learning more?

Wynn and I celebrated another anniversary. It seemed hard to believe that we had actually been married for two years. And yet, at the same time, I felt that the Elizabeth who walked the aisle of the little Calgary church on that day two years ago had been *so* young and naive. I had learned so much about life since that time.

Susie flitted through each summer day like a pretty little butterfly. She had outgrown her few dresses, and so I sewed her some more. I was careful to make them just like the dresses of the other children—no frills, no ribbons. I wanted so much to trim them up and make them feminine, like my niece Kathleen would be wearing, but for Susie's sake I did not. It wasn't that I feared Susie would not like the new attire. In fact, I was afraid she might like the frills too much and find it difficult to return to simpler clothing in the future.

But what of the future? The future looked bright. Maggie was much better, for which I was thankful, but certainly not well enough to care for herself and her family. I wondered secretly if I was also thankful for that, and hoped with all of my heart I wasn't that selfish.

Wynn took some longer trips to check on those who lived in his area of responsibility and yet were difficult to visit in the long, cold days of winter. When he went for overnight trips, I was even more thankful to have Susie with me. I didn't lie awake at nights worrying about Wynn and hearing strange noises around the house.

But just when I was feeling rather confident about the immediate future, my world came crashing down around me.

Susie had gone out to the garden to pick some lettuce for our lunch. I heard a shuffle at my door. At first I thought it must be Susie and Kip, and then I realized it was not the quick, easy movements which either the girl or the dog would be making. I turned from the tea I was brewing and looked toward the door.

It was the old woman, Too Many, who plodded in. She did not return my smile of greeting nor sit in the chair where she usually sat. Instead, she said slowly, brokenly, "Where Susie?"

I stopped and put down the teapot, fear filling my heart. Had something happened to Maggie?

I finally quieted my thudding heart enough to ask, "Is something wrong with Maggie?"

"Good," responded Too Many.

"The family?"

"Good."

I was relieved. So it wasn't some tragedy as I had feared. They probably wanted Susie to run a little errand.

"I'll send Susie down as soon as she comes in. She won't be long."

I wasn't sure how much Too Many understood. She knew very little English. I repeated the information as best as I could in her native language and with gestures, and she rose shakily to her feet and shuffled toward the door. As I watched her I wondered how the old lady could care for a sick woman, a set of twins, two lively boys and a senile elderly man.

Susie soon bounded in the door, Kip at her heels as always. Her face was flushed, her eyes shining.

"Know what?" she called to me as soon as she entered. "Soon we will have carrots. They are almost big enough now."

I looked at her, wondering if she was pulling up and replanting some of the vegetables again. She just couldn't resist seeing how big they were getting. Before I asked her, she looked at me, shaking her head.

"I didn't pull them up this time," she said. "I just scratched the dirt away from them, like this."

She showed me, with one wriggling finger, how she had taken her peek at nature's progress.

"Then I put the dirt right back again," she hastened to add.

I couldn't help but smile. I understood her impatience. I had been tempted to do the same thing myself.

"Hurry and wash, dear," I said to Susie. "Your mother wants to see you."

"Now?" asked Susie.

"Yes. I told Too Many that I would send you right away. I think you should eat first. They might have a job that will take you awhile, and you should have your dinner before you begin."

Susie ran to the basin, and I washed the lettuce and fixed our plates. It would be a hurried meal, but at least Susie wouldn't go to do her mother's bidding on an empty stomach.

We prayed together, ate our lunch, and then Susie was excused to run on home. Kip went to the door with her

"I think you should leave Kip this time," I said. "He might just get in your way."

Both Kip and Susie looked at me with pleading eyes, but I held firm.

"You won't be long," I encouraged her.

Susie gave Kip a goodbye hug and promised him that she would be back soon. Then she skipped out the door, careful to close it behind her as she had been taught at our house, and Kip turned whining to his rug before the fireplace.

Susie was back even before I expected her. She entered the house, her small face blank. Without a word she went to her bed and began to spread out the small blanket that she had brought with her when she came.

"Why the long face?" I asked teasingly. "Are you afraid you are back so soon that I will ask you to help dry the dishes?" Susie did not especially like to dry the dishes. Washing the dishes was fun—one got to play in the warm, soapy water. Susie would gladly wash the same few dishes all afternoon.

I turned, expecting to see a smile flit across Susie's face at the teasing, but instead I saw a silent little girl carefully folding her few dresses and other garments. She was making a neat little stack in the middle of her blanket.

"What are you doing?" I asked. When there was no reply, I answered for myself. "Is your mother now able to care for the family? Is Too Many going home?"

Susie shook her head.

"We go," she said simply, much like she would have said before she came to live with us and developed such good command of the English language.

"Go?" I echoed. "Go where?"

"To big village—cross the river."

"What?" I could only stand and stare, hoping I had not heard her correctly.

"Big village. They come in wagon—get us all. Take us to new home."

"There must be some mistake," I said, wiping my wet hands on my apron as I took it off and tossed it from me.

"No," answered Susie in a resigned little voice.

I didn't wait to hear more. I started for the settlement and the cabin across the little clearing, hoping to discover that Susie was mistaken. Susie was right. There was a wagon standing in front of her house. Two men were busy loading the few cooking pots and blankets belonging to the household.

Maggie sat in her chair watching, a smile on her face.

"See," she said in her own language when she saw me, "it worked. I prayed, they come. My brothers come to get me and my family, take us home to Father's house in big village."

It was plain to see that Maggie was rejoicing in the fact of the move. *But what about Susie? What about me?* I wasn't prepared to give her up yet. And Wynn? *Wynn is away. He won't even get to tell her goodbye.* My frantic thoughts tumbled over one another. Who would bring his slippers? Who would listen to his story? I wanted to argue with Maggie but there was nothing for me to say. Instead I said, "I'll be praying for you, Maggie. For you and each of your family."

Her eyes sparkled.

"They have church in big village," she told me. "He said so." She nodded her head at one of the men who was busy carrying out the last of the cooking pots. They were almost ready to go.

"I'll go get Susie," I said numbly, and hurried away.

Susie did not cry. Perhaps it would have been better for us both if she had. She just looked at me with those dark, soulful eyes. The pain and confusion nearly broke my heart.

I gathered her to me. "I'm going to miss you, Susie, so very much. I love you. Oh, I—" I couldn't go on. I knew I only was making it harder for both of us. "They are waiting," I finally managed.

Oh, why isn't Wynn here? Perhaps he could stop them— at least stall them while we sorted it all out. But Wynn was not with us, and he could have done nothing if he had been, my common sense told me.

Kip whined. I know he sensed something was not right. Susie reached out a hand to him and pulled him close, one fist buried in his deep fur coat, her other clasping tightly the little bundle of all her things. Still she did not cry. She held Kip for a moment and then turned and put her arms around my neck. She said nothing, just held me, and then she turned to the door.

She was about to close it quietly when she thought of something. She took one step back toward me, her eyes big and questioning.

"I took the dresses—was that steal?"

"No, no of course not. I made them for you."

She turned again to go, and then seemed to feel I needed to know something else.

She took a deep breath, looked into my eyes, then lowered them.

"I almost steal," she confessed. "When you gone, I almost put the book in my pack."

Her head came up and she looked at me again.

"Mr. Wynn wouldn't put children in jail. He wouldn't put me in jail. But Jesus—He would have been sad. He doesn't want stealers in heaven—so I left the book."

She turned to go.

"Susie, wait!" I cried, running to my little stack of books. I chose the three Susie loved the best.

"I want you to take these," I said as I hastened to shove them into an open corner of her little pack. "I want you to keep on reading. To think of us as you read the stories. To remember all the good times we had here."

Her eyes looked misty then. I thought the tears might spill over, but they didn't. "I remember," she nodded.

She was gone then, the door closing softly behind her. Then it opened again, just a crack and a small dark head leaned back into the room.

"I forgot thanks," she said humbly, and the door closed again.

I stood looking at the door. It didn't reopen. Kip whimpered and brushed against me. He wanted to go with Susie, and for one moment I was tempted to open the door and send him, to send the Silver One to take care of her, but reason kept me from doing so.

And then I let the hot tears stream down my face. She was gone. Just like that, our little Susie. Gone with her own people, back to her own world. Would she have a chance to be all the things I had dreamed for her? Would she ever be able to stand in front of a classroom? Would she be properly cared for? Would she have a chance to grow in her Christian faith? All these questions and more pounded in my brain, but all I could manage as I cried for Susie was, "She won't even get to eat her carrots!"

Chapter Twenty-one

Reminders

The silence roared all around me, deafening in its finality. Day after day I tried to adjust to being without Susie. Wynn eventually returned. He understood how I felt and held me as I cried. I believe he shed a few tears too over the loss of the little girl.

"We knew we'd have to give her up," he reminded me and himself.

I sniffed noisily. "Yes, give her up, but not so much 'up.'"

Wynn looked at me questioningly.

"I thought Susie would go back to her home here," I maintained. "I never dreamed that Maggie would move her away where we'll probably never see her again. I thought—I thought she'd just return home and she could still visit now and then, and I'd see her about the village, and she'd still come to school, and we'd work in the garden together, and—"

Wynn stopped me.

"We all thought that," he affirmed. "No one knew that Maggie had close family in the other village." He waited for a moment and then went on. "This is better for Maggie and her family. You know that, Elizabeth? They can be properly cared for now. Perhaps Maggie can regain her strength. Too Many tried hard, but she was an old woman. She had too much to do and too little strength to do it. I don't think they ate well. I—"

But this time I stopped Wynn.

"I know all that. I'm not sorry for Maggie—or—or for her family. It is best for her—and I've prayed—many times, for what was best. For Susie, too, I—I want what's best. I'm not crying about that. I'm crying about me," and the tears gushed out again.

At last Wynn got me comforted to the point where I could function, but I missed Susie dreadfully.

When the house was silent beyond my endurance, I fled to the garden. It was growing well. Susie would have been proud of her little patch. In spite of the attacks of mosquitoes and blackflies, I worked at pulling all the weeds. Then when I could stand the flies no more, I returned to the sanctuary of my quiet house.

Kip missed Susie, too. He seemed to be watching and listening constantly, his head cocked to one side, his ears thrust forward and straining. But Susie did not come.

Now the leaves went tumbling on the wind, wild geese honking as they passed overhead. I took in all of the produce from our garden. I gathered the produce from Susie's garden as well, sharing her vegetables with the people I knew to be her special friends. The men of the village prepared to leave for the traplines at the first fall of snow. I clanged the big bell and classes began again. This time five students came. The new interest was due to Susie's summer class sessions of play, I was sure.

We fell into a routine, and I was thankful for all the activities which filled my days. Still I thought about Susie. I thought about Maggie. Had I done enough? Said enough? Did Susie know how a Christian was to live out her faith? Did Maggie really understand about God's plan of salvation? Had I made it plain that it was for her, too? Had I really done what I could have, *should have*, done? Nagging thoughts picked away at me. I prayed and prayed for the family.

And then one day as I was praying, God spoke to my heart.

"Do you think I am unaware of where they are?" He seemed to gently say. "Do you think I have deserted them? Don't you think that I care, that my love is certainly as strong as yours? And don't you know that I, through my Holy Spirit, can go on talking to them, even in your absence?"

I felt humbled. Of course I knew all that. Maggie's salvation did not depend upon me. Susie's nurture did not depend on me. It had depended on God all along. Where they lived really had nothing to do with it. Now I committed them totally to God and let the guilt and fear slip from my shoulders.

I was still lonely, but the pain around my heart had eased. I visited Nimmie and some of the other women a little oftener to help fill the hours. Many of them began to drop in for tea again. Even though the fall days seemed to trudge along slowly, the calendar showed that our world was indeed continuing on.

In the midst of one of our first winter flurries, two Indian men on horseback approached our small cabin. Kip had alerted me, and I watched them as they came. One of the men dropped down from his horse, handed the reins to the other, and walked up our path to the door.

He bumped at the door rather than knocking, which sent Kip into a frenzy that I stopped by commanding him to go quietly to his corner. When I opened the door, the man reached into his leather jacket and withdrew a folded sheet of paper. He said not a word, just handed it to me, turned on his heel and went back to swing onto the back of his horse. Mystified, I watched them ride away.

The cold wind blew snow into the cabin as I stood there with the door open. Kip whined and I was jerked back to the paper I held in my hand.

I closed the door and went to the table, looking at the unfamiliar thing I held. I finally found my senses and spread it out on the table. It was a letter, just a simple letter written on a sheet torn from a child's work scribbler. There was no salutation at the top. It began with the message. I flipped it over and looked at the back side. It was signed "Susie."

My heart began to beat faster as I read. Susie's printing had improved; she had not forgotten what she had been taught. Hungrily I searched each word, each line.

"How are you. I am good. My mother is good two. We have a church here. I go. My mother gos two. We like it. We have a school here. Many boys and girls go. The teacher is nice, but not as nice as you. My mother feels better she says to say thank you. She didn't know before to say that. I miss you and Kip and Mr. Wynn. Did my garden grow okay. Susie."

I read the letter three times before I let the tears fall. She was fine! Our Susie was fine! She was in school, and in church, too. A little voice within me seemed to say, "See, I am caring for her," and I bowed my head in thankfulness to acknowledge that care.

Though the winter storm seemed to intensify, rattling the windows in its fury, it could not bother me. I felt warm and content. God was taking good care of our Susie.

Chapter Twenty-two

Sickness

Christmas came, a cold stormy day, and Wynn and I stayed indoors beside the fireplace, hoping he wouldn't be called out for some emergency. He wasn't, and we were thankful.

The next day was just as cold but this time Wynn was called upon. An elderly man, trying to gather wood in the storm, had fallen, breaking his hip. There was nothing much Wynn could do except give him something for the pain and try to make him as comfortable as possible.

Wynn talked to the family about trying to get the man out to the Edmonton hospital, but they would not even consider it. I fought my way through the storm with a pail of hot soup, which they seemed to appreciate.

Since I was out and already in the settlement, I decided to call on Nimmie. She was busy with her two little ones. Nonita, a cheerful little girl with an angel face that broke easily into a grin, was walking and trying to converse now.

Ian junior, whom they called Sonny, was not as cheerful nor as chubby. He had been a fussy baby from the first and did not seem to gain weight as he should. He was crying now as I was welcomed into Nimmie's home. Nimmie did most of her work with the baby cradled on her back or held in her arms.

Nimmie's face brightened when she saw me. "Whatever

are you doing out in this weather, Elizabeth?" she wanted to know.

"I came to bring some soup to the LeMores, so I decided as long as I was out I would stop by."

"I'm so glad you did," said Nimmie. "I needed someone to talk to." She smiled a bit ruefully and passed me the fussing Sonny.

"He has been so cranky. I think he must be cutting teeth. Nonita gave us no trouble. Even when she cut her teeth. She was such a contented baby, but sometimes I just don't know what to do with this one."

I walked the floor, patting his back and bouncing him up and down. He looked exhausted, but he couldn't seem to settle down to sleep. Nonita wanted her share of attention and ran to get her favorite book to show me the pictures. She jabbered as she pointed and I tried to reply as I walked back and forth across the wooden floor.

I had just gotten the baby to sleep when Nimmie said tea was ready. I didn't dare try to lay the baby down for fear he would waken, so I held him up against me and drank my tea with him in my arms.

Nimmie looked pale. I asked if she was feeling ill, and she just smiled a weak smile.

"Again?" I said in astonishment.

She only nodded her head.

Little Nonita tried to crawl up onto her mother's lap and Nimmie slid back her chair so she could lift the girl.

"I love my babies," Nimmie said, "and I am glad that another one is on the way, only this time I have been feeling so sick. I hope it passes soon. It is hard for me to care for the two of them when I feel as I do. Especially with the baby so fussy."

I felt sorry for Nimmie. I would have offered to take the baby home with me for a few days had Nimmie not been nursing him. "I could take Nonita if that would help," I offered.

"She's no trouble," Nimmie answered, cuddling the little girl she held.

"I'll come over and give you a hand here," I decided.

And so through the wintry months of January and February, I trudged off to Nimmie's almost every day where I helped with laundry, dishes and baby care.

On many days Nimmie was forced to stay in bed. She usually took the baby Sonny with her; cuddled up against her, he seemed to rest better. While they slept I did Nimmie's work and played with Nonita. What a little dear she was, and I found myself eager to get to Nimmie's each day just so I could spend time with the child.

At our supper table I shared with Wynn all of the funny things she said and did that day. We laughed about them together.

Being with Nimmie's babies did not lessen my ache for a child of my own but, rather, increased it. Each day I would petition God's throne for the child I still did not have. My heart grew heavier and heavier. It seemed I had been praying for a baby forever, and God still had not heard my prayer.

The first of March ushered in a terrible storm. The blizzard raged around us and Wynn did not leave the cabin. One could not see even a few feet in front of one's face.

I worried about Nimmie. Wynn reminded me that Ian senior would not be needed to tend the store on such a day, and he would be home to help Nimmie with the children. Although I knew Wynn was right, yet I missed my daily trip over to Nimmie's. Would Nonita be wondering where Aunt Beth was?

The storm continued for four days. I was sure we would be buried alive by the snow before it ended. What about those who had to get their wood supply daily? What would they be doing to keep warm? Wynn was concerned, too, and in spite of the weather he decided to see how people in the village were faring.

I hated to see him go. It was so nasty out and I feared he might lose his way in the storm. He took Kip, fastening a leash to his collar. He also took his rifle; he might have to fire some shots in the air, and I would need to reply with his lighter gun if he should get confused in his directions by the storm.

It seemed forever before Wynn was back. The news from the village was not good. Many people lay huddled together under all the furs and blankets they owned. Two elderly women had already died from exposure. In some cabins they had not been able to keep the fires going, and without fires there was no food, so those who were not well were getting even weaker.

Wynn said he was going to hitch up his dog team to haul wood to the homes where it was needed and asked me if I would take my largest pot and make up some stew or soup to be taken to the hungry.

I hastened to comply, my fears for Wynn's safety uppermost in my mind. It was risky working out in such weather. We both knew it, but under the circumstances it was the only thing that could be done.

It wasn't long until I heard Wynn and the complaining dogs outside our cabin. I knew Wynn was taking from our winter's wood supply to build fires in some of the other homes. If only the Indian people could be convinced to bring in a wood supply each fall and stack it by their doors. To them that was unnecessary work. The wood was always right there in the nearby thicket, they reasoned. I added some more sticks to my own fire so the stew would cook more quickly.

I bundled up and went with Wynn. It took me awhile to convince him I should, but at last he conceded. We carried the stew pot between us.

Wynn was right. Some of the people were desperate. While Wynn got the fire going in each cabin, I dished out some of the stew into a pot in the home and put it over the fire to keep hot. As soon as the chill was off the cabin, the people would crawl from under their blankets and sit around the fire to eat.

As we moved from cabin to cabin, we were thankful for

each one in which the people had been able to care for themselves. When our rounds were over, Wynn took me back home and then he set off again. He still had the two bodies to care for. As usual in our northern winters, they couldn't be buried properly till spring.

The storm finally ended and I breathed a sigh of relief, but it wasn't to be for long. With many people in a weakened condition, sickness hit the village. For many days and nights, Wynn worked almost around the clock. He gave out all the medicine he had and sent a runner out with an emergency call for more.

I made soup and stew, kettle by kettle, and we carried it to those who could not manage by themselves. We spoon-fed those too weak to eat alone. The homes were a nightmare of offensive odors, for there were no sanitation facilities and it was too cold, and the people too weak, to go outdoors.

I had to stop, pray and steel myself before entering many of the cabins. It was impossible to clean them up, though we did try, but illness soon had them in the same condition again. I was often glad for the mask Wynn insisted I wear over my mouth and nose. Though it did not shut out all the smell, it helped enough that I could function without getting sick.

The few who remained healthy helped us care for the sick. I don't know what we would have done without Ian, our faithful standby. He was always there, carrying wood and water and bringing food supplies from his store. And then Nimmie and her family became sick as well, and Ian was needed at home.

I called on Nimmie often. She was so sick I feared we would lose her. She did miscarry the baby she was carrying, but she fought tenaciously for her own life. Both the children were sick. I worried about the weak and sickly little Sonny. Surely his frail little body would not stand this additional illness.

But, strangely, it was darling little Nonita we lost. I would have cried for days had I not been needed so desperately. As it was I could only ache. *Poor Nimmie's little herb-gatherer, her little sunshine, is gone.*

When the sickness was finally conquered, the village had lost nine of its members. The rest of us were so exhausted, so empty, that we could hardly mourn. The bodies were all wrapped and placed in a shed belonging to the trading post—all except little Nonita. Ian spent many hours fashioning a tiny casket for her to rest in. Again, we would need to wait for spring before the burying could take place.

With heavy hearts we tried to strengthen one another. Nimmie valiantly braved her daily chores, but there was an emptiness in the cabin. She had looked forward to a family of three children, but she now had only one. Little Nonita's laughter and chatter was only a memory. I think Nimmie was glad even for Sonny's fussing. It gave her a good excuse to constantly hold him. Nimmie greatly needed her arms full during those difficult days.

Chapter Twenty-three

Summer of 'Fourteen

When spring came that year, I greeted the new life like old friends—tiny leaves, the flights of birds. I began to make plans for my garden.

Our classes of the year had been interrupted by the storm and then by the sickness. We missed nearly three months that should have been spent on the books. So we continued our studies a little longer than we normally would have. The village people agreed to it, I believe, out of gratitude to me. I tried not to take advantage of their goodwill and promised I would dismiss the children as soon as I saw that they were needed at home.

And so it was mid-July before we closed our school for the summer. I was ready for the break, too. With classes each morning, helping Nimmie and her little ones each afternoon in January and February, caring for the sick villagers for many weeks following that, and then trying to catch up with the schoolwork we had missed, I was exhausted. No wonder I was not expecting a baby, I told myself. My body was just too tired. In spite of my reasoning, my lack of motherhood still weighed heavily upon me.

I tried hard not to let my feelings show, but it wasn't easy, especially when I walked through the village and saw so many women who were with child. Why was it that I seemed to be the only one in the settlement who could not conceive?

One beautiful warm summer day, I decided I would fix a picnic lunch and take Kip for a long walk on the riverbank. Wynn was out on patrol and I was restless and lonely. I had just made up my sandwiches when there was a light rap on my door. Nimmie entered, her eyes shining, her cheeks flushed. She hadn't looked that well or that happy for months.

"Guess what," she said excitedly, but didn't give me any time for a guess, "we're going to have another baby!"

I was happy for Nimmie, really I was, but at the same time my own heart felt a pang of disappointment. Here it was again! I was called on to share the happiness of another when she was given the very thing I longed for so desperately.

I managed a smile and gave Nimmie a hug. I set aside my sandwiches and went to fix us some tea.

"I can't stay," stated Nimmie. "I left Sonny with Ian. The little rascal will be pulling things off the shelves. He's starting to walk now and is into everything. But I just couldn't wait to tell you. I know you grieved for Nonita almost as much as I did. It was so hard to lose her, Elizabeth. I thought I just wouldn't be able to bear it. And now God is sending me another child! I can hardly wait. This baby won't take Nonita's place, but it will fill a big emptiness in my heart."

It was the first Nimmie had really talked to me about losing Nonita. I knew that her heart ached, that she grieved. But she tried so hard to be brave. And now, as she said, the emptiness was about to be filled.

My emptiness remained. I turned so that Nimmie would not spot my brimming eyes and trembling lips.

"Are you sure you can't stay for tea?" I finally managed.

"I've got to get back."

She crossed the room to give me another hug, and I smiled and told her how happy I was for her, and then she was gone.

I didn't go for the picnic and walk after all. Instead, when Nimmie left I went to my bedroom. I cried for a long time before I was able to focus my thoughts and form words into prayer. My soul was still heavy when I finally pulled myself from the bed and went to wash my puffy face.

I took Kip then and went to the garden. I had just weeded the few weeds left in the garden, but I searched on my knees for any strays and pulled them with a vengeance.

When I returned to the house I still had not recovered from the heavy feeling in my heart. I prepared the same old supper meal I had been preparing for an eternity, it seemed. The same old blackflies and mosquitoes managed to find their way through any tiny chink in the cabin to plague me. The sunny day had turned cloudy and threatened rain. Wynn was late for supper and the meal sat at the back of the stove getting dry and disgusting. I was fighting hard to keep my emotions under control.

When Wynn did get home and stopped to rough-house with Kip and then came to greet me, I was rather distant and unresponsive.

"Something wrong?" he asked me, and I struck out at the first thing that came to my mind.

"How come the dog comes first?"

Wynn looked puzzled. "What do you mean?" he asked me. "When has the dog ever come first?"

"Now! Always! You always greet him before you kiss me."

It was a very silly thing to say. It had never even occurred to me before, but in my present state it loomed like a thundercloud.

Wynn took a moment to answer. Then he said, very softly and not accusingly at all, "That's because I can't get past him until I do. He's always right there at the door—"

I cut in, "And I'm not—is that what you're saying? The dog thinks more of you than I do?"

There was pain in Wynn's eyes but he was not to be baited.

"I'm sorry to be late, Elizabeth. I know it makes things hard for you."

I whirled around. "Do you think I care for a moment how hard and dry these old potatoes and carrots get? Or how cold and—and?" I dissolved in tears, turned from Wynn and ran to the bedroom.

I heard Wynn dishing up his own supper. I heard Kip coaxing for a sample of his food and Wynn telling him not to beg at the table. I heard Kip lower his body to his rug in front of the fire. Then I heard Wynn clear the table and quietly wash up the dishes. Still he did not come to me. Instead he took Kip for a walk.

They returned and I heard the complaint of the overstuffed chair as Wynn lowered himself into it. I heard his boots drop softly to the floor, one, two, and I knew Wynn hoped to be home for the night.

He'll come for his slippers now, I thought, and I turned my face to the wall and buried my head in my arms.

Wynn did come to the bedroom, but he did not bother with his slippers. Instead, he took me in his arms and held me close. He made no comment and asked no questions; he just held me and let me cry.

At last I was all cried out. Wynn kissed my tear-stained face.

"Want to talk about it?"

"It was silly," I murmured into his shoulder. "I really don't care if Kip—"

"No, not that. About what's *really* bothering you."

I played for time.

"The supper?" I questioned.

"Elizabeth," said Wynn, "I'm sorry about the dog; I'm sorry I was late for supper. But I don't think that is the real problem here. Something has been bothering you for days. I was hoping you would choose to share it with me, but you haven't. Can we talk about it?"

So it had shown.

"I guess the winter was rather tough—"

Wynn waited for me to go on but I didn't. Finally he prompted me.

"Are you saying you need a break?"

"Sort of . . . I—"

The silence between us seemed endless. Then Wynn spoke slowly, deliberately, "I can understand that, Elizabeth. I will see what I can do."

I jerked upright. "About what?" I demanded.

"About getting you out—back to Calgary for a—"

"I don't want to go back to Calgary. Whatever made you think—?"

"Well, Toronto then."

"Wynn, I don't want to go out—anywhere. That's not the problem."

"It's not?"

Poor Wynn. I had him totally confused. I looked at his anxious face, shaking my head slowly back and forth.

"Then what is the problem?" he asked.

"A baby."

"A baby? You mean you are going to have a baby?"

"No!" I cried, and began weeping again. "*That's* the problem. I want a baby—so much—we have been married for three years, and I still—" I broke off the sentence and threw myself into his arms, weeping uncontrollably.

We spent a long time talking and praying together that night. Wynn wanted a family, too. He had prayed about it many times. He was sure I would make a great mother, and every time he watched me with a child he felt sorrow that it was not our child I was holding.

"I still think you should get out for a bit," he told me. "You need to get to a doctor in the city. Who knows—I'll see what I can do."

"Wynn," I said, "I don't want to travel out with just anyone, not if you can't go too."

"I wouldn't send you with just anyone," said Wynn. "It might take a while to make the arrangements, but I'll work on it. Now and then Mounted Police personnel go through the area, or nearby. I'll see what I can find out."

My heart was really not that much lighter, but it did help to have shared my pain with Wynn. He'd be working on it. Perhaps the answer was near at hand.

Chapter Twenty-four

Waiting

It seemed to me that fall came awfully early that year, but perhaps this was because I knew I would not be going out to Calgary yet. Winter could come quickly to the land and stay for a long time, and Wynn and I had already decided that once there was a chance of my being caught in a winter storm when trying to get back to the settlement, I would not go. Now I would wait for spring and another year.

Heaviness hung about me as I gathered my garden vegetables and started the school classes again.

There were seven students now who were quite faithful. Wawasee still came—so that he could draw, but he now brought the younger members of the family, too. Jim Buck, my star pupil, rarely missed. Even teasing by the other boys did not keep him away. Two girls and a boy joined them. It really did seem like a school. They were learning well, and I was proud of them. As we got into the routine again, my despondency began to lift. My concern now was lack of material to take the youngsters further. I had to devise and make-do. Wawasee's drawing skills were a big help to me.

I thought of Susie. I still missed her. News from her village told us that she and her family were doing well. Her mother was feeling much better and was able to care for her own family. I was pleased for them.

The arrival of Ian's fall supply train created great excitement and anticipation, especially for Wynn and me. It meant letters and news from the outside world.

The news this year was not all good. The world was at war. This was hard for us to believe, tucked away as we were in our isolation. We pored over all the outdated papers that had been sent to us and tried to fit together the broken pieces of the world-affairs puzzle.

The war was across the great ocean and shouldn't have involved us, yet in one sense it did, for mankind cannot suffer anywhere without it bringing sorrow to other hearts. But the war was ours in another sense, too. Great Britain had joined the fight, and so would Canada if her troops were needed.

I thought of my young brother Matthew and prayed the war would end quickly. He was almost old enough to join, and I feared he might consider it if the fighting continued.

Most of the personal news was good. Julie was to be married—no, not the young officer with the Force; he had only been a friend. A young Calgary minister had won her hand and heart. Page after page was filled with her detailed description and her love and admiration for him. I was disappointed that I would miss Julie's special occasion but I was so happy for her.

Jon and Mary's family were all well and happy and growing steadily. Kathleen wrote a letter all by herself, telling me of her interests at school and her new cat, Bubbles. William, now a teenager, was a sports man, his favorite being football. Sarah, too, had grown up, proving to be quite a little seamstress under Mary's skilled tutelage. She was also studying the violin. "Baby Elizabeth" was almost old enough to begin school, and was constantly reminding the family that she was not a baby anymore.

Wynn's mother had not been well. I saw the worry mirrored in Wynn's eyes as he read the paragraph. However, Mary was quick to add, she did seem to be much better than she had been.

The wagon trains with the winter supplies and the mail had hardly been unloaded when winter sailed in from the Northwest. We all settled in, knowing that life would not be easy for the next several months. The men left for the trap-lines, the women took up their sewing, and the children played as they could between their duties of carrying wood and water. My students were not exempt. They too had responsibilities that must be attended to as soon as morning class was over. Therefore I never assigned homework of any kind. Our few hours together in the morning would be all the studying they would have.

Christmas, for a change, was a beautiful day. The temperature was cold, but the wind was not blowing and the sky was clear. We decided to go for a walk in the snow. Kip blocked the door, his tail wagging furiously as soon as he sensed that something out of the ordinary was happening. He wanted to be sure he would not be left behind.

I did not pack a lunch. We had no way to keep it from freezing, and on such a chilly day a frozen sandwich would not be too enjoyable.

We bundled up against the cold and laced on our snow-shoes. I'm sure every member of our small village would have thought us extremely foolish to be setting off through the deep snow when we did not even need fuel or water.

It was a beautiful walk. We saw several deer and admired their gracefulness. We did not need the meat, so they were in no danger from us. The beaver pond was almost totally iced over except for a small hole they somehow kept open. We did not see the beavers but it was obvious they had been around recently. Some young poplars were newly cut and the strange tracks, with the dragging tail, were clear in the fresh snow.

We could tell it was getting chillier by the time we returned to the cabin. The warmth from the fires felt good as we removed our heavy outer things. I fixed us some hot chocolate and sandwiches. Then we curled up on the rug before the fire and read to one another.

It was an enjoyable Christmas Day. Then I thought of the pleasure of having a little one sitting between us, but I pushed the thought aside. I would not let it spoil our time together. I'd try to be patient as I waited. It wouldn't be long until spring and then Wynn could start trying to make arrangements for me to see a doctor in the city.

One blustery March afternoon I welcomed Little Deer in for tea. She had not been over for some time, and when I saw her I understood why. She was large with child. Though she did not say so, restlessness and boredom with the waiting had driven her from her cabin. We talked in her native dialect—fortunately for me, fairly simple in structure. Now and then I still needed to search for a word, but I could converse quite freely with the women.

"How soon—your baby?" I asked her.

"Soon now—too long already," was her answer.

She sipped her tea.

"How many now?" I asked.

She held up her fingers, like a child. "This makes five—two gone, two stay, and this."

I understood. She had lost two children, had two at home and this would make three.

"I'm happy for you," I said, smiling.

She looked a bit doubtful. "You like babies?" she asked.

"I love babies," I was quick to respond.

"Then why you not have some?" The question was abrupt, direct, and Little Deer's black eyes searched my face.

Panicked, I stammered and searched for words. How could I answer her? What were the Indian words to tell her that God had not seen fit to bless me with a child—yet? That I needed to see the city doctor to find out what was wrong. What should I do? I was still trying to sort it all out when Little Deer spoke again.

"When we do not have a baby, we go to Big Woman for good medicine. It make baby come."

My eyes must have opened wide and my mouth dropped open. Did the Indian people really have medicine to help with a pregnancy?

"Does—does it really work?" I asked, forgetting myself and switching to English, then having to repeat it in Little Deer's language.

"Good," she said with emphasis. "It work good. You get the medicine, pay Big Woman, you have a baby. Like that." She gave a little wave of her hand to show just how easy it really was.

My head was spinning. Surely—surely, there wouldn't be any harm in paying Big Woman for a little medicine. If it didn't work I wouldn't be any worse off than I was now. It was likely some special herb. The Indian people knew of many good herbs to help all kinds of things. I would ask Nimmie.

Now I was anxious for Little Deer to finish her tea and depart for home. I wanted to rush right down to Nimmie's to find out about Big Woman's special medicine. When I finally was able to get to the trading post, I tried hard not to be too eager. Very casually, I thought, I led the conversation around to the herbs of the Indian people, of which Nimmie was very knowledgeable. Then I said, as though it was of no special import, "Little Deer was in for tea this afternoon, and she said that Big Woman even has a medicine to help women conceive."

I waited, my heart thumping. Nimmie made no response.

"Is it true?" I prompted her.

"Partly," said Nimmie.

"What do you mean, partly?"

"There's a little ceremony that goes with it."

"What kind of a ceremony?"

"It's a little song, or chant."

"Do you know the words?"

"I don't think anyone but Big Woman knows the words."

I wanted to ask more, but just then Sonny pulled the dish of cookies onto the floor before either of us could make a grab for it. Nimmie sat him in the corner and was cleaning up the mess when a strange look came over her face.

"What is it?" I asked, worried that she might have hurt herself in some way.

She straightened slowly.

"They have been coming and going since noon. I think that it is time, Elizabeth."

I didn't stop to ask her more but ran through the side door into the store. Ian went to get the midwife, and I ran back to assist Nimmie into bed.

"I'll take Sonny home with me," I assured her. "Just as soon as Ian and the midwife get here."

She was one of the two in the village. When she arrived with Ian, I recognized her at once as Big Woman. She took over with a great deal of authority and assurance. I watched her as she set about making Nimmie comfortable. While she worked she talked to Nimmie in a soothing sing-songy voice. Was this what Nimmie meant by a chant? Her old face, lined with wrinkles, seemed to be void of all expression.

I bundled up the small Sonny and bid Nimmie goodbye. I hoped it would not be long until we heard good news. I thought Nimmie was probably hoping for another little herb-gatherer, though she had not said.

We had finished our supper when Ian came for Sonny, his face broad with a grin.

"Another boy," he beamed. "Alexander." And I wondered if Nimmie shared his great joy. Then I decided that she certainly would. She would welcome whom God chose to send.

How I envied Nimmie with her new son. There hadn't been a chance to ask her if she had ever tried any of Big Woman's medicine in her long years of waiting for a child. I wanted to ask her, yet I was hesitant.

Something about the whole idea troubled me. Yet what harm could it possibly do?

Chapter Twenty-five

Temptation

Through the following days I continued to think about Big Woman and her medicine. Wouldn't it be wonderful if I could find help right here in the village and not need to travel way to Calgary, leaving Wynn behind? I wanted to talk to Wynn about it, but something I couldn't identify always held me back. It seemed so reasonable to go to see Big Woman. Yet something made me uneasy whenever I made up my mind to go.

I visited Nimmie and her new baby frequently. He was a lovely, healthy boy and seemed to have grown each time I went to see him. Alexander was a contented baby with a chubby little face and dimples. His dark eyes watched your face and his small fists knotted themselves at the front of your gown. I loved him, almost like he was my own.

I held him and thought of the sweet little Nonita and my heart ached. Was it possible that in the days ahead fever again might strike the village and this one, too, would be taken? *Does Nimmie ever think these thoughts?* I wondered. *Maybe I should be glad that I've never had a child.* I didn't think I could stand to have one and then lose it. I couldn't imagine anything harder to bear.

But Nimmie made no reference to fear. Daily she thanked God for her new baby and for the fact that Sonny was healthier than before. He still was small for his age and seemingly fragile, but he was active, and he was not the fussy baby he had been.

I never did find the courage to ask Nimmie if she had been to see Big Woman. It seemed too private a thing for me to ask.

I did ask Nimmie what she thought of Big Woman as a midwife.

"I have told Ian that I would prefer Kantook, but if she is busy, Big Woman is fine."

I later found out that when Ian had gone looking for Kantook, she was already busy delivering Little Deer's child, a boy, too. So two new braves were added to the village that evening.

Nimmie's answer had not really told me what I had wanted to know, so I pried a little further.

"In what way is Kantook better?"

"I didn't say she was better," said Nimmie.

"Then what did you mean?"

"I really don't know how to explain it to you," said Nimmie. "I guess one could say that Big Woman is the 'old,' Kantook is the 'new.' "

It sounded reasonable enough, but I still didn't know what Nimmie meant by it.

With the coming of spring, I knew Wynn would be searching for a way to get me out to Calgary. If I was really serious about seeing Big Woman, I would need to do something quickly.

I thought of just getting up my nerve and going on my own, without even mentioning the fact to Wynn. Then if Big Woman's medicine did not work, I would be the only disappointed one. A nagging little voice inside told me that would not be right. Wynn should know what I was planning. I broached the subject one night after we had retired. I found it easier to express myself in the dark, when Wynn could not study my face.

"Little Deer was over for tea one day a while back," I began, "and happened to mention that there is a woman in the village who has special herbs to help one to—to—" I faltered some. I wasn't sure just how to go on. "For those who do not have children," I finally said.

Wynn made no reply, though I knew he was carefully listening to every word I said.

"She said she has helped women here in the village."

"Who is it—this woman?" asked Wynn.

"She's one of the midwives."

Before I could even name her, Wynn said, "Big Woman?"

"Yes. You knew about it?"

"No, but I'm not surprised."

"What do you mean?"

"Big Woman will promise anything for a little money."

I was a bit put out with Wynn. Didn't he think a baby was worth a little money?

"City doctors want money, too," I reminded him.

"But they're not witch doctors," Wynn stated simply.

"Big Woman is a witch doctor?" I was astounded.

"Hadn't you heard? She practices all kinds of witchcraft when she has opportunity. We try to discourage it, but we can't control it altogether."

I sank back against my pillow. In my desperation I had nearly consulted a witch doctor. I had rationalized that a little chant could do no harm. Yet I knew with all my heart that any kind of witchcraft or sorcery was wrong. No wonder I had felt uneasy! And then, much to my dismay, I realized that in the days and weeks I had considered going to see Big Woman, I had not once prayed about it, asking God what He would direct me to do.

If I had prayed, if I had just prayed, I would have known. Yet even in my ignorance and my own waywardness, God had protected me from going.

I humbly closed my eyes and offered up a contrite prayer. I would not try to take matters in my own hands from now on. I would leave it to God. And if I was to go out to see a proper doctor, I would trust Wynn to make the arrangements.

And then I poured out the whole story to Wynn, telling him about my desperation, my temptation, my holding back, and now my deep thankfulness for being kept from perhaps bringing into our home a child who had been conceived through witchcraft.

Chapter Twenty-six

Duty

Spring was slow in coming. Just when I was beginning to hope, another storm would strike. The sun made no visible headway on the hip-deep snowdrifts, and the icicles on the eave troughs grew and grew.

I suppose I was more anxious for spring than ever, once the idea of going "out" had taken root. I also was looking forward to seeing family and friends again. So I chafed with each new flurry that came our way.

One afternoon, just as another swirl of snow began to cover our little settlement, Wynn returned to our cabin, his face set in a grim expression. I knew something serious had happened. He did not bother to play with Kip, but pushed him aside and came to me.

He kissed me first and then spoke, his voice grave. "I have just gotten word, Elizabeth, that someone has been trading illegal liquor to our Indians. I don't know who it is or where he is working, or if there is more than one. But I have to go check it out."

He kissed me again and released me to go and pack his gear. I followed him, not knowing what to say or to do. He was preparing much more carefully than usual.

"How long will you be gone?" I asked him, able at last to find my voice.

"I have no idea. I wish I could say it will take only a day or two, but the truth is, I have no idea how long it might take."

"Are you taking some men with you?"

"No, I will be going alone."

"But why? You might need help. The man, or men, might be dangerous."

"That's true. That's why I am going alone. This isn't the kind of thing that you can ask others to share. It's the law that is needed here."

His words frightened me and brought a chill to my heart. His trail gear caused me further fear. Never had I seen Wynn take such pains. He made his list and double- and triple-checked it, making sure he had everything. The amount of ammunition also frightened me. Did he think he might need it? Were whiskey runners really that dangerous? Yes, I had heard enough stories from others to know that indeed they might be.

"What can I do?" I asked him helplessly. "Will you want to eat before you go?"

Wynn gave me a rather absent-minded smile. "Great idea," he said; "something hot would be good."

I left him and went back to my kitchen. The fire was burning well and it did not take me long to have a hot meal for Wynn and a pot of strong tea.

When he came from his office, I was ready. He noticed just the one plate on the table. "Aren't you going to join me?" he asked.

"No, I—I'm really not hungry. It's only three o'clock."

"How about a cup of tea then?"

"It's stronger than I like it."

"You could water it down some."

I shook my head. I just didn't feel like putting something into my churning stomach.

Wynn studied my face, but said nothing more.

"Is there anything I should do while you're gone?" I asked, feeling helpless and lonely already.

"Just take good care of yourself! I have left word with Ian to keep a close eye on you. If anything is needed, you be sure to let him know."

Wynn finished his meal all too quickly and was pushing away from the table.

"I'm going for the team," he told me. "I will load up here. You might watch Kip. I don't want him slipping out the door and tangling with the sled dogs."

I nodded and mechanically began to clear the table.

Wynn was not gone long. I could hear the yipping and complaining of the dog team as they made their way to our cabin. I wondered if they were thinking the same thing that I was—that this was a strange time of the day to be taking to the trail. I had thought of asking Wynn to wait until morning but I checked myself. If Wynn had not felt it was important to leave immediately, he would have decided to sleep at home and strike out on the trail early the next day.

It did not take Wynn long to pack. I helped only by carrying some of the gear to the door of the cabin. Wynn himself had to arrange and pack the sled. He would want to know exactly where everything was located.

I determined not to cry as I said goodbye, but it was difficult. I reminded myself over and over that Wynn had gone on dangerous missions before and always returned.

We prayed together before he left as we always did, each of us imploring God to protect the other. Then our door was closed and I heard Wynn's voice commanding his dogs to be on their way.

I did not go to the door or a window. I did not want to see the snow flurries blot him from my vision. Instead, I went to the bedroom to spend some more time in prayer.

I will confess that I did shed a few tears as I prayed, but when I came out of my bedroom it was with renewed peace of mind and a determination to use, rather than waste, the days that Wynn would be gone.

The first thing I did was to get out the stew pot. I had heard that one of the elderly couples in the village had not been well. I would take them something nourishing.

By the time I returned from my trip to the invalids, it was already dark. I was glad for the warmth of the cabin as I entered and for Kip who met me at the door. I tried to play with him in the same manner Wynn always did, but it just wasn't quite right, and Kip backed away from me with a puzzled look in his eyes.

I fixed a plate of stew for myself and took it and my tea to the chair before the fire. I wasn't hungry. I ended up scraping my stew into Kip's dish for him to finish.

If only there was some way of knowing how long it would take Wynn to locate and apprehend the criminal. I did hope and pray there wasn't more than one of them.

I mended a pair of Wynn's socks and a tear in one of my slips and then turned to a well-read book. I had read it so often I was sure I could have recited it by memory, but I couldn't concentrate. I decided to go to bed early. Maybe the night would pass quickly.

It didn't. I lay awake listening to the storm. The wind was stronger now. I pictured Wynn out in the open somewhere, trying to get some sleep in the cold, wintry night.

Kip was restless, too. He kept moving from his fireplace rug to my bed, and then back again. I was about ready to get up and shut the bedroom door to keep him in one place, and then I realized he would only sit outside my door and whine and that would be even worse.

The night finally did come to an end, but the new day was not much better. After I dismissed my morning class, I went to visit Nimmie to help her with her little ones. She really didn't need my help that much. She had everything well under control, but she humored me by finding small jobs for me to do.

I trudged home through more flakes. Would it never stop snowing?

Kip met me at the door, excited about my homecoming. I fixed some supper and gave Kip his evening meal and wondered how in the world I would fill the long evening ahead.

It seemed forever that I went through a similar daily routine, but the calendar on the wall told me it was just six days.

Ian was the one to bring the news. When I saw him coming toward the cabin, his long strides eating up the snow-covered ground, my heart filled with fear. Did he have bad news? He walked so purposefully.

But when I opened the door, Ian was smiling. "An Indian trapper just stopped at the Post and said that Wynn is on the way in. I thought you'd like to know."

I thanked Ian, my glad heart rejoicing. He was finally coming home!

"Did he say how long it will be?" I asked.

"Should be here in a couple of hours. He's bringing a prisoner, so he sent word for me to have the cell ready."

A prisoner! Then Wynn had found his man.

Ian turned to go and I went to prepare a meal. Suddenly I felt very hungry and I was sure Wynn would be hungry, too.

It was a little more than a couple of hours before I heard a dog team enter the settlement. I could tell by the strange yip of his lead dog, Flash, that it was Wynn's team. I looked out the window. I had to scratch a spot in the frosted pane in order to see.

I could just make out Wynn's tall form in front of the Post. After commanding the team to lie down, he was ushering a man into the building. I knew he would care for the team before he came to the house, so there would still be a wait.

I could hardly contain myself. It had been so long, and I was so glad to see him safely home again. I wanted to throw on my parka and run down to the settlement to join him. But I knew Wynn would have things to attend to before he would be free to come home for his supper and a much-deserved rest.

I don't suppose it really took Wynn all that long to do what had to be done, but it felt like a lifetime to me. Then at last I saw Kip leave his place by the fire and press his nose hard against the door, and I knew Wynn was on the way.

This time I did not wait by the stove, letting Kip get first greeting. I ran to the door and threw it open and even before Wynn could step inside I was in his arms.

He looked very weary, his face drawn from exhaustion. I did not hold him at the door long, but pulled him inside. I helped him remove his heavy mittens and parka, the whole time telling him how relieved I was to have him home again. Kip kept telling him that, too, with joyful little yips and great tail wagging.

It wasn't until Wynn crossed to his chair to remove his heavy boots that I noticed the limp.

"What happened?" I asked in alarm.

"I'm fine," he replied. "Nothing to worry about."

"But you're limping."

"A little."

"Is it your foot or your leg?"

"Leg."

"Wynn," I said, exasperated, "what happened?"

"How about having some supper, and then I'll tell you all about it?" said Wynn. "I'm absolutely starved."

I hurried to the stove to dish up our meal. I would not ask Wynn for more until he had eaten.

I never did hear "all" about Wynn's experiences. What I did hear was enough to give me chills.

Wynn started his hunt by going to the cabin of a trapper who was reported to have purchased liquor from the trafficker. Wynn found a very sober Indian, his head in his hands. Empty bottles were strewn about his cabin. There were signs that he had been sick from the alcohol. "Gone," he groaned out to Wynn. "All gone. All my winter's furs, all gone." He had traded some of the furs for the whiskey, and then when he was too intoxicated to defend himself the lawless trader had slipped away with the rest of them.

Wynn had gone on, following the fresh trail. He found another trapper in much the same condition. Wynn pressed on. Soon he found a third. This man was still out from the liquor, and Wynn knew the trail was getting hot. However, he could not leave the Indian until he was sure he was sober enough to care for himself. The weather was still cold enough that one could freeze to death if left unattended.

This delayed Wynn and he had to really push his team when he got back on the trail.

The next cabin made Wynn realize just what kind of a man he was looking for. The trapper had apparently refused to trade his furs for the whiskey. Wynn found him dead from a gunshot wound through the heart, and the cabin was stripped of furs.

Now Wynn knew he was up against not only a thief but a murderer as well. He knew also that the man would stop at nothing. It was imperative that Wynn get to him before more lives were lost.

Wynn pushed the dog team for most of the night to close the gap between himself and the man. The storm had finally broken, and the moon gave enough light for Wynn to see his way.

Near morning he stopped for some rest, more for the dogs than himself, and then he was on his way again.

He overtook the man about noon the next day. He had stopped for a meal and had built himself a little fire for a hot cup of tea. Wynn approached cautiously, leaving his team fanned out in the snow over the hill away from the man.

When Wynn got in close to the man's camp, he called to him. He told him who he was and that he was coming in to get him.

The outlaw called back, "You've got me, Sarge. I know when I'm licked. But at least let me have a cup of tea to thaw me out a bit before you run me on in."

Wynn stepped out into the open and approached the man slowly. He was almost into the camp when the man swung around with a hand gun and took a shot at Wynn, just missing as Wynn dived into the snow.

From his concealed position behind a bank of snow, Wynn

watched the outlaw. Wynn was afraid to take his attention off him for fear he would make a run for it. But the man preferred to stay close to his fire, confident that a Mountie would not shoot to kill if there was another way.

The sun went down and the moon came out, big and bright. The man fired at Wynn just often enough to hold him at bay. All night long they lay on the snow, challenging one another, but the trader had the advantage of a small fire.

In the morning, before the sun returned to the sky, Wynn could sense that the trader had plans for some new deception. Wynn decided that he must move first and so he did. He worked himself around slowly in the cover of the snowbanks and spruce trees until he was no longer in front of the man, but to his left side.

Wynn could tell that the man was preparing for travel. Knowing that time was against him, he made a dash for the camp, hoping to catch the man off guard.

The plan worked. The surprise rush gave Wynn just enough time to shoot the gun from the man's hand as he swung around to meet him. There was a price to pay, though, for as the trader's gun went off the bullet caught Wynn in the right leg, causing a painful flesh wound.

Wynn didn't say too much about what happened after that, but somehow he managed to get the bootlegger in cuffs and extract from him the locations of the trappers he had dealt with.

There were two others besides the ones Wynn had already seen, and with the illegal trader leading the way, Wynn traveled to those cabins to check on the men. At the first cabin they discovered a very angry Indian man who himself had been tramping the woods looking for the trader. Wynn assured him that justice would be done, and sent him to recruit the help of another nearby trapper to transport all the stolen furs back to the village where they would duly be returned to the rightful owners.

Then Wynn and the arrested man went on to the last victim. It was as Wynn feared. The trapper, in his drunken condition, had been unable to keep his fire going and had frozen to death in the sub-zero weather.

Wynn tied this body, too, on his sled and, with the two dead men and the outlaw in handcuffs, he headed back to the village.

Now the prisoner was in the security of the Post jail. Wynn told me he would spend the night at home and then set out to bring the man to Edmonton.

I protested. He was in no condition to travel again so soon, I told him, but Wynn waved aside my concern.

"Elizabeth," he said, "that man is deadly. Never in my years of law enforcement have I met a man as cold and calculated. He would stop at nothing."

I was sure Wynn was right and that only increased my fear.

Wynn did allow me to nurse the angry red wound in his leg. I was afraid it would become infected, but Wynn poured on medicine that made him wince with the pain and assured me it would heal just fine. He did, however, take more of the disinfectant with him when he left the next morning. I didn't know if that was a good or a bad sign.

My greatest fear was for Wynn's safety. The outlaw had already proved that he had no regard for human life. What was to stop him, in his desperation, from attempting to kill the man who was taking him in? Surely he would do everything in his power to avoid being tried for the crimes he had committed. Wynn, with little sleep and an injured leg, was at a disadvantage.

I spent a restless day and a sleepless night, praying for Wynn's protection. I was glad when morning finally came and I could crawl from my bed and try to find something to occupy my hands and mind. I was more than eager to bang the school bell that morning, and called the children a bit early to class. Their presence would help fill the emptiness of the cabin.

I was mentally prepared for many sleepless nights and worry-filled days, but, much to my relief, Wynn was back that next evening. He had met two members of the Force who had been sent out from Edmonton to help with the man-hunt.

I was grateful to have Wynn back home again and glad that he had not had to travel all the way to Edmonton on his bad leg. He had been told by the man in charge of the mission to rest for several days, and he took his advice—at least for a few days. Then he was up and about, anxious to have more to do than catching up on his paper work. Soon he was back out among the villagers again, his limp barely noticeable.

Chapter Twenty-seven

Out

The two trappers who had picked up the stolen furs had brought them in to Ian's trading post, and Wynn oversaw the sorting of whose furs were whose. I couldn't see how the men could tell one fur from another and asked Wynn about it.

"Oh, they know their own furs all right, no problem there," said Wynn. "Little marks or nicks or coloring. They can identify them all."

The furs of the dead trappers were traded in at the Post for the families of the men. Wynn told me that Ian had given them more than a fair price.

All the village men returned from their traplines, and then I knew that spring really had returned.

We finished up our classes, and I started to work on my garden. I was glad to have my hands back in the soil and to watch things begin to grow. A few of the other women in the village had seen the advantages of a garden, and Nimmie and I had been happy to help them get their own started.

I was just settling in to another quiet summer day when Wynn came back to the house.

"Are you all packed?" he grinned, and I looked at him questioningly.

I knew Wynn was still trying to find a way for me to travel

out of Edmonton, and then to Calgary. For several reasons, I was anxious and chafing to go, and yet at his words now, a strange little reluctance raised its head.

"What do you mean?" I asked him.

"I heard of a party going out, so I sent a runner to ask them if they could drop by this way."

I didn't say anything.

"If they come, they should be here sometime tomorrow. I expect that they will spend the night here and then move on early Thursday morning," continued Wynn.

Thursday morning. Excitement and doubt filled me at the same time. Could I really leave Wynn for several weeks with no means of communication between us?

Wynn pulled me close. "I'm going to miss you, Elizabeth," he said, taking for granted that I would be going.

I sniffed. "Who is it?" I asked, almost hoping it would be someone whom I could refuse to travel with.

"A couple from the Force. I didn't discover their names."

Members of the Force! I could hardly refuse to go with them, if they would have me.

"Are you sure they'll be willing to take along a woman—?"

"I think they will. Most of us try hard to accommodate one another. We need to help each other in any way we can. I'll send along a small tent for your use. They won't mind setting it up for you."

I sighed. "Then I guess I'd better get ready," I said reluctantly.

"I guess you had," replied Wynn, and he kissed me on the nose and then went back to his work.

I was suddenly in a frenzy. I hauled out my wardrobe and realized that I didn't have a thing decent to wear. Whatever would I do? I had no time to make anything and no material to do so, even if there had been the time.

I hope no one sees me before I have a chance to get to a store and make some purchases, I thought frantically.

Yet I wasn't as concerned about my own preparations as I was about Wynn. I did his laundry, although I had done it all just a few days before. I baked some fresh bread and some cookies and a cake. I made up some stew and sealed it in jars so that he could heat it as needed.

In a fever pitch, I worked all afternoon and the next day until in the afternoon I heard the sound of many barking dogs in the village.

I rushed to the window and looked down toward the settlement and found that the visitors had come. The men traveled in a wagon with a pair of tired-looking horses, thin and ill-kempt from the long winter.

I could see even from my vantage that they wore the stripes of the Mounties. I saw Ian's hand raise and point in the direction of our cabin, and then the wagon rolled on toward me.

I had no hay to offer them for their horses but told them they were welcome to let them graze on the tall grass out back of our cabin, provided they kept them well away from my garden. The shorter one grinned at my comment and went to care for the horses.

I invited them in to have a cup of coffee and some fresh bread and they seemed to like the idea. They were still at the table when Wynn came in. He had heard they had arrived and hurried home to have a chance to visit with them and to catch up on any pertinent news.

"So what takes you out?" he asked them. "New orders?"

"No," said the taller one known as Hank Lovess. "The war."

"They haven't settled it then?" was Wynn's response. "I was hoping by now it would be over and done with."

"Guess that's what we'd all hoped, but 'fraid it ain't so," said the shorter one, Ted James. "From the reports we been gettin' it might be lastin' awhile yet."

"So you're joining up?"

"Gonna do what we can," said James.

Again I thought of Matthew. If this horrid war continued, would he go? A chill gripped my heart.

The men talked on, but I went outside to the clothesline

to get Wynn's things so I could iron them. I didn't want to hear about the war anyway.

Wynn took the two men for a tour around the village while I prepared supper. I was relieved to have them out from under foot, and then I remembered that I would be "under foot" for them for the next several days. I wondered how they felt about that.

Just as Wynn had supposed, the men stayed overnight. They declined our offer to sleep on the floor in the cabin and spread their bed rolls out under the tall pine trees. Perhaps they knew Wynn and I needed this time alone. There was so much to say to one another and yet words were so inadequate. We talked on until late into the night, yet I can't remember one thing of importance that was said.

Morning came all too early. The men were anxious to get on the way, and I was determined not to be any more of a nuisance than was necessary. Wynn held me for a long time before we went to join the men, yet it wasn't nearly long enough. *When will I see him again?* my heart wailed as my eyes searched his face one last time. He was sending a letter to Headquarters asking that when members of the Force next traveled back our way, I would be contacted and given opportunity to travel with them. That might be in a few days' time, or several months—I did not know.

The trip out was not too difficult—probably because I was better prepared and knew what to expect. I was busy counting off the days until we would be in Edmonton.

The men were not talkative. They did not even converse with one another. I guess they were both used to silence.

I tried to help out where I could, but even the cooking they did better than I, being more used to the trail and open fires.

The nearer we got to Edmonton, the more my blood began to race. I was going "out." How different would the world be from the one that I had left behind? How much change would there be in my family? *How much change will they see in me?* I wondered as I looked down at my faded, patched dress and rough hands.

When we reached Edmonton, the men arranged for my stay in a hotel, purchased my train ticket to Calgary and told me how and when to be at the train the next morning. I thanked them for their kindness, and then with a lump in my throat, I wished them well in the war they were going to fight on behalf of myself and the rest of Canada. They had been good to me, these young gentlemen. They had not fussed nor pampered me, but they had been kind and patient. I assured them that my prayers would follow them.

I was on my own then. *On my own in a big city—I wonder if I still know how to act?*

I asked for help from the man behind the desk and set out, embarrassed about my attire, to find the nearest dress shop.

After doing enough shopping to at least get me to Calgary in a somewhat presentable state, I went back to my room.

What *plush accommodations!* I exulted. A soft carpet covered the floor, and lacy curtains, overhung by thick draperies, graced the window. The room was as large as our kitchen-living quarters, and then some. I hardly knew what to do with all that room to myself.

I went into the bathroom and gasped in amazement at what at one time I had taken simply for granted. It had been years since I had seen such luxury. I crossed to the tub, my fingers caressing the smooth white surface. The towels were so soft they felt like Kip's thick fur, and the room smelled as fresh as a pine forest.

I ran the water, pouring in a generous supply of bubbly soap and then submerged myself in the warm, soapy water. It felt so good! I stretched out lazily. *What a treat to get all of me in the tub at the same time!*

I don't know how long I spent in the tub. I only know that by the time I reluctantly crawled from it, my fingers were all wrinkled and the water was quite cold.

I wrapped myself in my worn old robe, thinking ahead to

the soft fluffy one I had left behind at Mary's. It would be good to see my fashionable clothes again. The soft things, the dainty things, the pretty colors, the frills and foibles. I could hardly wait. I had missed them.

I dressed in my simple new gown. It really was quite becoming. I carefully did my hair up in a way I hadn't combed it for ages. When I was done I surveyed myself in the mirror and was pleasantly surprised at how good I looked.

Then I looked down at my hands and saw the stains and callouses from working in the garden, peeling vegetables, washing clothes on the scrub board, and I hid my hands behind me. I was no longer the cared-for and manicured girl who had left Calgary for the wilderness a few years earlier. I hoped no one would look at my hands. And then I noticed my arms. They had a number of telltale little welts on them, each indicating a spot where a mosquito or blackfly had visited me. I knew my face and neck bore the same spots, and my confidence began to quickly wane.

Then I straightened up to my full height, reminding myself that I wasn't "out" to set the fashion world to buzzing. I was here to see my doctor—to get some answers, to get some help. And, just as quickly as possible, I would be rejoining my husband in the North where I belonged.

With those thoughts to bolster my courage, I left my room and went down to the front desk to ask the attendant where I might find the dining room.

Chapter Twenty-eight

Calgary

The next morning as the train left the Edmonton depot bound for Calgary, I was almost giddy with excitement. I would soon be seeing my family again! I would be back to the city life I had once known. And, more importantly, I hoped to get some help from my doctor.

The train had not changed. It was still ponderously slow and stopped at every little siding to waste some more precious time. I could hardly bear the agony of it all.

At long last we came to Lacombe, and I strained to see if I could catch a glimpse of faces that I might know. Though the streets of the little town were busy, I did not see anyone whom I had known while a teacher there.

At long last we were on our way again, chugging south, the tracks clicking as we made our slow progress.

Again it was stop and go, stop and go. The sun swung around toward the west, hot as it came in the window. I wished for a seat on the other side of the aisle, but the train was filled with passengers. I shifted farther away from the window and tried to keep from looking out to determine just how far along the tracks we were.

It was no use; I was soon crowding the window again, straining to see out and to guess the distance left to Calgary.

We finally reached the city, and I held my excitement at

bay while the train pulled into the depot and with a giant sigh, shuddered to a halt. I remembered well the first time I had entered Calgary. The city had changed much since then, but I had changed even more. The young, stylish school-teacher from the East no longer existed. In her place was an older, wiser and, I hoped, more sensitive woman.

Jon's entire family was there to meet me. I had called them from the Edmonton hotel the evening before, telling them I would be arriving by train. They were almost as excited as I was. How the children had grown! I couldn't believe how tall William was—and how mature-looking for a mere boy. He was a teenager now and hoped everyone would realize it.

Sarah, too, had shot up and looked like a young lady rather than a child. She was now eleven and carried herself with an air of grace.

But I suppose that it was Kathleen who had changed the most. From the dear little child of four who had met me at the station and become my constant companion, she was now a young nine-year-old girl, poised and proper. I fell in love with her all over again, though I found it difficult not to wish the little girl back again.

Baby Elizabeth, who had been only a few months old when I arrived in Calgary the summer of 1910, was now ready to start school in the fall.

Mary had the same bright smile, the same beautiful reddish hair, the same flashing eyes I remembered so well. Jon had not changed much either, although I noticed a few white hairs in his carefully trimmed sideburns.

I looked around for Julie. I guess Mary could read my mind.

"Julie is out of town. Her husband is taking some services at Lethbridge and Julie went with him. We phoned her last night and she was so excited she could hardly stand it. She was going to hop the train and come right on up, but he will be finished tomorrow and then they will both be home."

I understood, but it would be hard to wait.

I hadn't remembered that Jon and Mary's beautiful home was so big. Nor so lovely. I wandered around, running my hand affectionately over furniture and fancies. I had almost forgotten that such things made up a house—at least some of them.

Dinner was delicious. We had dishes that I had not tasted for years. Wonderful Stacy had prepared all my favorite things—stuffed chicken breasts, whipped potatoes, creamed broccoli, corn on the cob, and for dessert her famous chocolate mousse. I ate until I felt ashamed of myself.

All the time I was enjoying Mary's home and Stacy's dinner, I thought of Wynn. *If only he were with me—this would be sheer heaven!* But Wynn was far away in his northland. A little ache tugged at my heart.

Back in my old room and after soaking in a luxurious bath, I reclaimed one of my lacy, silk nightgowns. Feeling much the pampered lady, I climbed into bed, smiling to myself in the darkness. The bed was so soft and smelled so good that I had visions of the best sleep I'd had for years. But it didn't work that way. I had become used to a harder mattress. I tossed and turned but sleep did not come. Around three o'clock, in desperation, I threw my pillow on the carpeted floor, took a blanket with me and lay down to sleep.

I felt foolish curled up on the carpet and fervently hoped I would waken in the morning before I was discovered. I was soon asleep.

The next day was busy. I got out all my stored dresses and admired their beauty as I pressed them ready for use. I had forgotten I had so many pretty things. I did need to do some shopping, however, so in the afternoon I took the street-car downtown.

I had felt sophisticated and proper when I left Mary's house, but I hadn't been on the streets for long until I realized that my beautiful gowns were now dreadfully out of style. The farther I went, the more evident it became. I certainly didn't have the funds for a complete new wardrobe, yet it was plain to see that the dresses of today were far different from mine; I stood out on the streets as one who had been clothed from missionary barrels supplied by the castoffs of the rich.

In embarrassment, I headed home.

I was hardly in the door when I told Mary, "My dresses are dreadfully out-of-date. What will I do? I had no idea that the styles have changed so much."

Then I looked more carefully at Mary. If I had been observant, I would have noticed yesterday that she, too, dressed in the newer fashions.

"Oh, my," said Mary noticing my discomfiture, "I should have thought to tell you, Elizabeth, but you always had such pretty things."

"Well, they might be pretty, but they definitely aren't in vogue. I don't want to buy a new wardrobe for the few days I will be in the city, and I don't have the money for that even if I did wish to. But I will need something else. Most of the dresses on the street were much shorter, and not as frilly, more—more tailored looking. And my hat—it was all wrong, too."

"Why don't we see what we can do?" offered Mary. "If you don't mind them being cut, I'm sure we can find ways to change your dresses and make them quite acceptable."

"They are no good to me as they are. If you can fix them, even two or three of them, I can make do."

We chose three dresses that seemed to lend themselves to change and then dear Mary set out to alter them. They turned out quite well, and I felt that now I could walk the city streets without too much embarrassment. Jon and Mary added a little surprise. They asked if they could take me shopping for a new suit and hat, with shoes and bag to match. I hesitated at first, but when Mary expressed her love and deep desire to do this, I consented, and gave them both a big hug.

Julie finally arrived, running quickly up the front walk. She was bubbly. She was beautiful. She was in love. And she was noticeably pregnant. My breath caught in a little gasp.

"I wouldn't let Mary tell you," she enthused. "I just had

to tell you myself. Oh, Beth, I never knew just how happy one could be."

I hugged her close. I was happy for her, too, and no one there knew that the tears on my cheeks were more than just shared joy for Julie.

We had a lot of catching up to do. Her eyes shining with love, she proudly introduced her young husband. I remembered that Julie had once swooned over Wynn and had asked me if the Force had any more like him. Well, Reverend Thomas Conway was not another Wynn. He was much shorter and slender in build. He had rust-colored hair, with a carefully trimmed little mustache to match. He had laughing deep blue eyes and a kind smile. He looked like just what Julie needed, and I liked him immediately.

Julie insisted on sharing her wardrobe for the time I would be in Calgary and brought over three dresses that fit me just fine. Actually, she couldn't wear these particular ones in her condition anyway, she assured me. With six dresses, a suit and proper shoes, hat and bag, I felt quite confident to face the world.

I smiled to myself as I hung up the garments. *Imagine the Beth of old wearing hand-me-downs, made-overs and garments of charity!*

We called Toronto on Jon's telephone and I had a long talk with Mother and Dad, their voices bringing back so many memories. They were alone now. With the older girls married and scattered, me up north, Julie out west and, as I had feared, Matthew gone to war, there were just the two of them.

Mother was worried about Matthew and I'm afraid I was no comfort to her. I was worried about him, too. I thought about this young brother, a man now, who wished to serve his country, and a little prayer went up even as my chest constricted. *Why did he have to go?* I asked myself. But I knew. He went for the same reason so many other young men were going. Their country needed them.

After the first few days of flurry and bustle had passed, I

decided I was now ready to phone the doctor and make my appointment.

Mary immediately became concerned when I told her that my real reason for making the trip was to consult a doctor. But when I hastened to explain that, no, I had not been ill, not more than an occasional cold or flu the entire time I had been in the North, she relaxed. I was having a checkup at my husband's request, I informed her, and she agreed that it was a good idea and Wynn was right to desire it.

The doctor visits and tests were soon behind me and the day came for my final consultation. With anticipation and fear I went to see him.

He was a balding, elderly man, his understanding eyes almost hidden behind bushy eyebrows and dark-rimmed glasses. He motioned for me to be seated and cleared his throat.

I nervously twisted the handkerchief I carried, my eyes studying his face for some clue. I wanted so much to hear good news.

"Well, Mrs. Delaney," he said, clearing his throat again, "all the tests are in now, and"—he hesitated for what seemed like forever and then went on—"I find no reason for you to not conceive."

I exhaled and let my body relax.

"That's good news," I said in almost a whisper.

The doctor looked over the glasses. "That depends on how you look at it," he said. "If we don't find a problem, then we cannot do anything to correct it." He cleared his throat again.

He waited for my reaction, wondering if I had understood what he had just said.

I understood what he was saying. *There is nothing he can do for me. I might as well not have come.* It really made no difference. No difference at all.

The good doctor continued talking, explaining things I did not understand, but then I was not really listening. I had already heard all I needed to know. Now I just wanted to get out of his office.

I went for a long walk before catching the streetcar home. I don't really know where I went, I just walked, not paying much attention to where I was going or what was around me.

I came to the river, and as I stood gazing down on it my mind began to clear of its fog. Perhaps the river reminded me of the wilderness. It was the only thing in the city that looked like home.

I lowered myself to the grassy bank in the shade of the poplar trees and let the tears flow. I wanted Wynn. With all my heart I wanted Wynn. No one else really understood how I felt. I cried for quite a while before I got myself in hand. Then I blew my nose, dipped cool water for my face and went in search of a streetcar.

Mary and I had a long talk that night. I told her all about my problem, my aches, my longing. She understood as well as another could understand. She promised that she too would pray that my desire would be granted. I appreciated her love and understanding and encouragement, but I still felt empty.

Besides, I felt threatened by this strange world I had come back to. All the talk of the war, the daily news of more conflicts, the lists of those killed or missing in action filled the papers and caused an atmosphere of constant fear. I didn't feel comfortable with this new world. My northern isolation had protected me from all this.

I got in touch with Headquarters for any information on when I might be able to return to the North. The man with the deep bass voice told me that there was nothing he knew of in the immediate future, but that he had my number and strict orders to contact me as soon as something came up.

I thanked him and hung up the phone. I did pray, with all my heart, that it would be soon.

Chapter Twenty-nine

Home Again

Three weeks, and still I had not heard from the Force Headquarters. At night I thought I could not stay for one more day. The days were a little better. I found many ways to fill them. I went for walks with Kathleen, inspected Sarah's sewing, took shopping trips with Julie and had long talks with Mary.

My greatest joy was the Sundays. I enjoyed more than I can tell being back in a church service. I guess that was when I missed Wynn the most. I kept thinking how much he would appreciate the services, too.

In spite of my loneliness for Wynn, I was glad to be home again. I even took a trip to Lacombe and spent some time with Mother Delaney and Phillip and his family. I was relieved to find Wynn's mother doing much better. Wynn would be glad for the news.

While I was in the area I visited Anna and had coffee and some of her delicious Swedish baking. We drove by the school and I saw they had added another room onto the little teacherage. I was so glad to see that school was continuing.

As I visited I was often reminded of why I was "out." Repeatedly, inquiries were made about my "family" and though the questioners were asking out of interest, I found the remarks deeply painful.

In spite of the delights of the city, I chafed inwardly. I was lonesome for Wynn. I even felt a little homesick for the North. I was beginning to understand how Nimmie had felt. It seemed that I had been out for such a long time. Surely there must be someone from the Force heading north. What if they had forgotten me? What if someone had already left and now I must wait for many weeks more? Should I phone them again or would they think me a nuisance?

I longed for Wynn. I longed for Nimmie and her babies, for the Indian women who came for tea, for the sound of the wind in the pines and the smell of wood smoke in the air.

I longed for Kip, pressing his cool nose into my hand, coaxing me to stroke the softness of his beautiful coat.

I was homesick. I was miserable. And no matter how hard I tried to be agreeable and enthusiastic about all that folks were doing for me, the ache never left me.

At long last, two men were being dispatched to a post near our area, and they would accommodate me in their travels. I had three days to get ready. I could take along 100 pounds of baggage, no more, and should be ready to leave on Wednesday's train.

I was beside myself. *I'm going home!*

The time was spent gathering and packing, weighing and repacking. I wanted to take supplies for my school and books were so heavy. I sorted and pondered, resorted and packed nearly half a dozen times.

When it came time for me to dress for the train trip to Edmonton, I again had trouble deciding, *What should I wear?* The new suit would be ideal for train travel, but would not be of use to me in the North. Yet to wear one of the simple dresses I had purchased to take north with me would look absurd.

Mary solved my dilemma. "Why don't you wear the suit, hat and shoes, and when you get to the hotel in Edmonton, just send them all on back to us in this little case?"

I did.

I dreaded all the goodbyes, but I was so anxious to be on

my way that I did not linger over them. I held my little Kathleen longer than the other children, perhaps. It was hard to leave her again, knowing that the next time I saw her, she might be a young lady. Then it was all over and we were on the train, moving ever so slowly toward Edmonton and the river that would take us on the first leg of our journey north.

I tried to relax, but every nerve seemed to be straining forward. The time would never end.

The days on the trail were no better. I joyfully greeted each familiar landmark. It was the thick cloud of mosquitoes that first welcomed me back to the northland. I swatted at them and smiled to myself. I would soon be home.

The men were kind. One of them was a little too kind, I thought, and took every opportunity to offer his extended hand, or assist me up or down or wherever. I avoided him as much as possible.

At last we left the river, too, loaded the waiting wagon and started up the trail that would lead to the Post.

We camped for the last time, the men setting up my tent before building the evening fire. I was walking about, studying the clear night sky and wondering how on earth I could endure another day on the trail before I would see Wynn when a figure moved toward me in the semidarkness. I would have recognized the stride anywhere, and with a glad cry I ran to meet him.

Wynn had heard we were coming and had come to meet us. We held one another tightly while the tears coursed down my face. Oh, how I had missed him! I would never be able to tell him just how much. For now I was content to be held closely. For the first time in weeks the little gnawing pain was gone from my heart.

Proper manners demanded that Wynn greet the other Mounties and spend some time catching up on the outside news. I wanted him all to myself but I held myself in check.

There would be many days ahead for us to catch up on everything.

The next day as we walked along behind the wagon, Wynn
and I talked about all the things that had happened to each
of us while we had been apart, except I said nothing about
the doctor's report. I was afraid it might bring tears with the
telling, so I wanted to be in the privacy of our own home
before I reported to Wynn. He, wisely, did not ask. Instead,
we talked about the family, the villagers, the war, and what
we had seen and done during the weeks apart.

Many people from the settlement came out to meet us. I
was deeply touched that they should care so much. I greeted
them by name and was pleased to discover I had not forgotten
the difficult Indian language I had picked up over the years.

We trudged on the last mile together. A warmth and close-
knit feeling seemed to hang in the air all about me. As we
neared the settlement the smell of the wood smoke hung in
the air. I sniffed deeply. I had missed it. In the distance I
could hear the gentle roll of the river, and nearer at hand
the soft whispering of the wind in the pines. I put my hand
in Wynn's.

"You wouldn't believe," I murmured, "how wonderful it
is to be home."

Wynn squeezed my hand and pulled me closer to him. I
could see by the shine in his eyes that he was just as happy
as I.

Chapter Thirty

Settling In

The little cabin we called home looked tiny and simple after being in Mary's lovely home. But I looked around at the bear-skin rug before the fire, the shelves that held my dishes and supplies, the table where we sat to partake of venison stew and biscuits, the home-made pillows on the cot, and I felt at home again.

The first day was a busy one. Though I was tired from the trip, I could not rest until I was sure that everything was spotless and orderly.

As soon as the sun was up I ran down the little path leading to my garden. Wynn had kept it weedless while I had been away. I couldn't believe how much it had grown. The rabbits had been raiding again. I could see where they had nibbled off many of the plants.

My next errand was to get Kip. Wynn had left him in the care of Jim Buck. He seemed as pleased to see me as I was to see him. I thanked Jim, and Kip and I ran the short distance home together.

During the morning Wawasee came, bringing his most recent drawings for me to see. I smiled my approval, and spoke very slowly in his native tongue so he could follow me by lip-reading.

"I like your pictures, Wawasee. I brought you a picture

193

book from the city. You must come back to look at it as soon as I get unpacked. In the morning—in the morning I should have it for you."

He beamed and I knew by his shining eyes that he would be back in the morning.

In the afternoon several ladies came for tea. They did not all come together but in twos and threes. I would no sooner clear away the cups from one group than another would be at my door. I was soon caught up on all the village news.

I had seen Nimmie briefly the night before, but I was longing for a good chat with her. My first day was too busy to arrange for that chat. I still needed to unpack my things so the book would be there as promised when Wawasee came the next morning.

I cooked Wynn a special supper that night. It wasn't stuffed chicken breasts and creamed broccoli, but I took special pains with what I had on hand.

I settled back into the routine of village living with a light heart, except for the news from the doctor that I shared with Wynn.

I continued to argue with God. Didn't Hannah receive the child she had prayed for? Weren't there numerous women in the world who had children which they did not really want nor care for? Did the whole thing seem reasonable? Why shouldn't those who would love and protect the child be the ones to give birth? Why not me? Why should I be denied?

I tried to push the thoughts from me, but daily they nagged at me, eventually making me nervous and listless. I lost weight. I did not sleep well. I found no answers.

I had been home for two weeks. I felt again the peacefulness of the little settlement, but I had been wrong about one thing. I had thought that in leaving behind the newspapers, the radio and the war-talk, I could shut out the fact of the war. With Matthew somewhere in the fighting, that was impossible. My thoughts and prayers often were of him and the other sons who had gone to fight. I thought of the parents, the wives, the sweethearts whom these men had left behind and I prayed for them also. Especially did I pray for my own mother and father as they waited out the long, long days for Matthew's safe return.

It was beginning to look like fall again. The sun spent fewer hours in the sky, the leaves turned to yellow-gold on the poplars, the birds gathered in the trees, calling to one another. Our garden was full-grown and tasty. It would soon need to be gathered into our storage room. We started our school again.

One day Wynn came to the cabin in the early afternoon. I looked up from the bread I was kneading. He had not planned to be back until the supper hour, so I knew something had happened to change his plans.

"Remember the young woman who had the baby boy about ten days ago?" he asked.

I nodded. The couple was new in the village and I did not know them well.

"She's not well. I've just been over to take her some medicine again. Do you think you could check on her in a short while? Maybe take her something to eat? Her husband is away, and she is all alone."

I promised Wynn I would go just as soon as I prepared the food.

The young couple had built a new cabin on the edge of the settlement, and I hurried there with my soup and bread. There was no response to my knock on the door, and then I remembered that she likely did not know what a knock meant. I opened the door and went in.

On the corner bed I found the woman, weak with fever. Her forehead was very hot. A tiny baby lay against her, sleeping contentedly. I checked the water pail and found that it had just been refilled. Probably Wynn had done that when he had looked in. I didn't know whether to try to get her fever down first or to feed her some nourishment. I decided to sponge bathe her.

I spoke to her in her own language, and I could see a response in her eyes.

"How long have you been sick?" I asked her.

"Not know—many days have gone."

"Where is your husband?"

"In big village."

"Do you know when he will be back?"

"Not know."

She didn't seem to cool much with the bathing, so I gave up and began to spoon some of the soup into her mouth. She was able to swallow the food, for which I was thankful. I then gave her a piece of bread and she fed that to herself.

It was then that the baby stirred and began to whimper. I reached down and picked him up so I could comfort him and check his condition.

There was nothing wrong with him except that he was in desperate need of changing. I took care of that and cradled him for a moment before I placed him back beside his mother so he could nurse.

He did not appear to be suffering even though his mother was ill. He looked filled-out and healthy.

"I will go now," I said to the young woman, and left her to see if I could find Wynn.

Wynn was not hard to find. He was checking a winter supply list with Ian. Medicines were number one on his list.

"How is she?" he asked as soon as I entered.

I frowned, concerned. "Not good, Wynn. She is so hot. I'm afraid she is very ill. Do you think you should send for her husband? She says he is at the big village."

"I've sent for him. It'll be three days at best before he gets here, and if he is hard to locate, perhaps many more."

"I don't think she should be left there alone, Wynn. Is there a way that she could be moved to our place so I could care for her properly?"

Wynn thought about it.

"That will be a big job, Elizabeth—and what about your school?"

"We'd have to cancel classes for a few days, but that wouldn't hurt. It's more important to try to get her well."

"I think we could find a way to get her there."

"I'll go get the cot ready."

It was not long until the woman and her baby had been bedded on the cot in our living quarters. Most of the time she slept, restlessly tossing about in her fever. I bathed her often, trying to get the fever down. I was afraid that in her tossing she might injure the baby, so I had Wynn bring in a crate and we made him a comfortable bed.

For the next four days all my time was spent caring for the mother and baby. I would just begin to think there was some improvement, and then she would get worse again. At times she could not even nurse her child. I had Wynn bring some canned milk from the store and we fixed a makeshift bottle to supplement his feeding. On the fifth day the worried-looking husband came to our door. He crossed quickly to the side of his wife's bed without even exchanging greetings with me. She was a bit better, and I was glad she recognized him. He went to the crate and picked up his young son. He seemed pleased that the child fared well. It was only then that he turned to me and spoke, "I take them home now," he said.

I wanted to protest. The woman was not fit to be moved, but I knew better than to argue. I just nodded my head in agreement.

He left for some help and was soon back with two other men to carry the woman on a blanket and pole stretcher to their own cabin. The baby was crying as they left. He was hungry and the woman no longer had much milk.

I worried about them. For the first few days I would drop by to check on them. The husband always greeted me at the door and said that mother and baby were "good." He was caring for them. From the smells coming from the cabin I knew that he was doing some cooking and was feeding her. He seemed to be responsible. I would have to leave the matter with him.

One day as I walked to the store I met Big Woman coming from the new cabin. She was carrying a strange-looking leather pouch. I had not seen her with it before.

She gave me a toothless grin, her face softening in wrinkles.

"She get better now," she said. "I make strong medicine."

I didn't know what she had done. Probably one of the chants that Nimmie had spoken of, and it had likely cost the young brave much of his hard-earned money. I felt sorry for the family.

When the days passed and there was no news of the family, I dared to hope that things had improved. Wynn still visited the cabin. He continued to give the medicine he had on hand, but that did not seem to stem the fever either.

One dark evening as we sat before our fire expecting the night to bring the winter's first snowfall, there was a shuffling at our door. Kip ran to welcome whoever it was, with Wynn close behind him.

It was the young man. In his arms he carried the baby boy. He nodded solemnly to Wynn and crossed the room until he was standing before the cot where I sat.

"You take. Keep," he said, holding the baby out to me. "She gone now. I go trap."

He placed the baby in my arms which had raised automatically to receive him, and then spun on his heels and was gone.

I stood staring after him, not knowing what he meant or what I was to do.

The door closed softly and Wynn was beside me.

"What did he mean?" I asked, my voice full of wonder.

"He lost his wife," said Wynn.

"But the baby?"

"He has to go to his trapline. He wants you to keep the baby."

Tears began to trickle down my face. I cried for the young father. His eyes were filled with pain as he handed me his child. I cried for the mother who had fought so hard but had died so young. I cried for the baby who had been left motherless at such an early age. And I cried for me, tears of joy, because I now held a baby in my arms, a baby to love and care for. I held him close and thanked God for answering my prayers.

We named the wee baby Samuel. It seemed fitting. Hannah had named her baby Samuel after God had answered her prayer. The name meant "asked of God," and every time I said the name I was reminded again of the miracle of Samuel coming to us.

He had lost weight since I had last seen him. I knew that his poor sick mother had not been able to feed him properly. I was not alarmed. He seemed healthy, and I was sure he would gain rapidly when given proper nourishment.

My days were so full that I scarcely had time to have my morning classes. For the first few days I often sat and sewed while the children studied, as Samuel had very little to wear. My pieces of soft yard goods were finally being put to use.

At first Kip seemed a little jealous of all of the attention the little one was getting, but then he too seemed to decide that this little bundle must be pretty special. He took to guarding the cradle, fashioned lovingly by Wynn out of packing crates. Kip did not allow even the ladies who came for tea to go near the baby until I commanded him to let them.

At first Samuel had a great deal of catching up to do. He slept and ate, making up for the time when he had not been properly fed. He soon rounded out and as he regained his strength, he also became more aware of his surroundings.

It wasn't long until he was smiling and cooing like any normal baby. He was so easy to love. He made our little cabin a place that was alive and warm.

When winter came, I scarcely noticed the storms. I was too involved with my baby. Kip did not get his exercise as faithfully. I was much too busy and Samuel could not go out on the colder days.

Nimmie provided me with a cradle board to fasten Indian-fashion on my back with Samuel held securely in place, so when I did take him out for fresh air, it was not difficult for me to carry him.

Christmas was the best one we had ever had. Wynn and I spent many evenings making toys for Samuel. We could hardly wait for Christmas morning to arrive. Samuel rewarded our efforts with squeals and chuckles, and we felt that we had discovered what Christmas was really meant to be.

That Christmas our prayer time was thoughtful and filled with devotion. It meant even more to us now to read that God gave His Son—*His Son*—to bring eternal life to the world.

We had been so busy enjoying Samuel that I had not thought about his age. Suddenly one day it hit me: I did not know his birthday. I was anxious to ask Wynn. The Indian people in our village paid little attention to the day of their birth. To know the season of the year seemed to be close enough. "I was born at the time of the coming of the geese," or "I was born at the time of the heavy snow," but not, "I was born on May 15" or "on November 21."

When Wynn came in that night and headed right for the cradle and a squealing, arm-waving Samuel, I expressed my concern.

"We don't know Samuel's birthday," I said. "That might be important some day, when he registers for school or—"

"That's easy to find," said Wynn. "I keep a record of all of the births and deaths in the settlement."

We went to Wynn's office together, Kip trailing along behind. Wynn passed Samuel rather reluctantly to me while he got out a thick record book. He ran his finger down a column and came to, "infant boy born to Little Fawn and Joe Henry Running Deer, August 15, 1915."

"That's a strange name," I said.

"Whose?"

"The father's."

"They often combine English and Indian names."

"Yes, but not with two like that. A middle name. Henry. Joe Henry."

"Ian said a white trapper by the name of Joe Henry used to live near the big village. He said that the Indians thought highly of the man, and several of the young men were named after him."

As I looked again at the page and Wynn's recorded announcement of the birth of our small Samuel, another little pain went through me. Again I felt sorrow for the young man and woman whose home had been struck by such tragedy.

I carried the baby back to the living quarters while Wynn put the record book safely away.

"We'll try to make it up to you, Samuel," I whispered. "We'll care for you and love you, and when you are older we'll tell you all about your mother and father. They loved you, too, you know."

I kissed his soft, dark cheek and laid him back in his cradle so I could get supper on. He didn't stay there for long. Wynn was soon back and giving him horsey rides on his bootless foot.

Chapter Thirty-one

Spring Again

Never had the trees looked so green or the breeze sung so softly. With spring, the birds returned, and I held Samuel up to the window so he could see their bright feathers and hear their twittery songs.

He was crawling now and pulling himself up to stand on two rather shaky legs. He no longer fit his cradle, so Wynn again went to the packing crates for more lumber to make a bigger bed. It hardly fit in the small room, and we were tempted to move the cot out. Instead, we squeezed things in as best as we could—there was very little room for walking around.

The men came back with their winter furs, most of them having had a good year. The pelts were plentiful, thick, and brought good prices. I shut my eyes against the vision of the small helpless animals caught in the cruel traps and thought instead of the better food and clothing that the winter's catch would bring to the families in the village.

I watched, without really admitting it to myself, for Joe Henry Running Deer. I thought he might come to see his son, but he did not. I did not even see him in the village. Wynn thought of it, too, I guess, for he remarked one night that it appeared Joe had returned to the big village and that the cabin was now going to be used by another young man and his new bride. It was an unwritten law in the village that when a cabin was not occupied, it could be used by someone else who needed it.

I took Samuel out more and more as the weather warmed. He loved the out-of-doors. We took long walks with him riding in his special carrier on my back. We went to the river, down forest paths, to the village—all over our home area. And as we went I talked to Samuel, in English and in his own language. Wynn and I both encouraged him to try new words in each tongue.

In the evenings I read to him or showed him picture books. I sang him little songs. First I sang to him the songs my mother had sung to me when I was a child, and then I had Nimmie teach me the songs she sang to her little ones so Samuel would know them, too.

We visited Nimmie and her children often. Samuel loved other children. He would smile with delight whenever he saw Nimmie's boys. They loved him, too, and they had a wonderful time sharing toys on the floor while Nimmie and I sipped our tea and watched them with eyes of love and pride.

We sent word out to our family and friends, telling them of our son. I suppose I did boast a bit, but probably no more than most new mothers. Back with our infrequent mail came parcels and well-wishes. Now Samuel not only had handmade toys but commercial ones as well.

When it came time for the spring planting, I set Samuel on a fur rug while I worked in my garden. He played in the soil, letting it trickle through his fingers. I watched him carefully for a time, to see if he would try its taste. He didn't, so I left him happily playing and went on with my work.

When I checked on him only a few minutes later, he had not only tasted the dirt but he seemed to enjoy it. His chin was covered with mud from the mixture of dirt and dribble. He grinned at me happily as though to say, "Don't get alarmed. No baby has died from eating dirt yet."

I picked him up, wiped him off, scolded him as a matter of course, and placed his rug on the grass instead.

We closed the little school for the summer and I had more time to spend with Samuel. He was taking a few faltering steps now. Wynn and I spent our evenings together coaxing him to walk between us. He seemed to sense he was doing something pretty special, and he would squeal to be sure he had our full attention each time he took a step.

Much of my time was taken with sewing new garments. Samuel outgrew his things so quickly. I wondered how Hannah ever managed to get by with one small new coat a year. I smiled as I thought of the mother-love that must have gone into that one new coat.

One thing plagued me. Samuel was growing up so quickly, and I would have no pictures of him as a baby. I knew that in years to come the pictures would be very special—not just to Wynn and me but to Samuel himself. I tried to think of ways to get the use of a camera, but I could come up with no good solution. And then I thought of Wawasee. Samuel and I went to see him, and I explained to the young boy what I wanted and promised him all the scribblers he needed if he would draw several pictures of the baby for me.

Wawasee seemed to think this was a strange request. He was used to drawing wild animals and birds, or dog teams, or men fishing. But he didn't argue. He set to work sketching Samuel. At first he seemed a bit awkward and the pictures did not turn out well, but as he worked he began to get the feel for it. Soon he was producing very good likenesses of the baby.

He came often after that and spent hours sketching the little boy, sleeping in his bed, playing with his toys, burying his face in Kip's thick fur, feeding himself his mashed vegetables. All of the pictures caught the spirit of the baby Samuel. As I looked at them, I knew I had a treasure far beyond what a mere camera could have given me.

Chapter Thirty-two

The Birthday Party

Samuel's first birthday was drawing near. I was busy trying to come up with ideas that would make it a special occasion, but I hadn't made much headway. I decided to discuss it with Wynn. I waited until after Samuel had been tucked in for the night and was sound asleep.

"Samuel will be one on Saturday," I informed Wynn.

"I remember," he said. "I've already picked out his gift."

My eyes widened. "You have? What?"

"Not telling," Wynn said with a grin. "You'll just have to wait and see."

"Wynn," I pleaded, "that's mean."

But Wynn only laughed.

"Well, you've already got your gift. I've seen you sewing on that stuffed horse for days," he said.

"Shhh," I cautioned, casting an apprehensive eye at the bed in the corner, and Wynn laughed harder.

"I would like to make his birthday really special," I went on.

"For Samuel—or for you?" Wynn said, his eyes twinkling.

"For all of us," I stated, a bit annoyed at Wynn's teasing.

"I'm sure the day will be special, just because we are together. But what would you like to do?" Wynn asked, becoming more serious.

207

"That's the problem. I still haven't thought of anything."

"Then might I give you my suggestion? I think it might be fun to pack a lunch and take our son on his first trip into the wilderness. We could spend the whole day—take Kip, our birthday dinner and make a whole day of it."

I loved the idea and began at once to think of the things I would need to prepare for the backpack birthday dinner.

Saturday dawned fair and bright. I went early to the kitchen and began my preparations for the dinner we would carry with us. Wynn had already left the cabin but would be back soon for breakfast.

Samuel awoke and pulled himself up in his bed, his face crinkled up to cry until he saw me nearby. Then he began his chattering to tell me that he was hungry and ready for another day.

I went to him and lifted him up, kissing him on the cheek.

"Today is your first birthday," I informed him, but he didn't seem too excited about it. "We are going to take a long walk in the woods, Daddy and Kip and you and me. We'll see all kinds of things that you should know about. Beaver dams, animal tracks, different trees and birds, and Daddy will tell you all about them."

Samuel was interested only in what was for breakfast.

I dressed the baby and went back to the kitchen just as Wynn arrived. He had his hand tucked inside his tunic and a funny grin on his face. "Is it time for birthday gifts yet?" he asked and I laughed at him. He was even worse than I was.

"Okay," I agreed, my eyes on Samuel, "but you have to wait until I get mine."

I went to the bedroom and brought the small calico horse I had made, entering the room with it hidden behind my back, and then while Samuel sat with a bewildered look on his face, Wynn and I sang "Happy Birthday to You."

"You first," said Wynn, and I pulled the toy horse out from behind my back and kissed Samuel as I presented it to him.

He reached for it with a smile on his face and stuck one small hoof into his mouth.

"No," I told him. "It's not to eat. You're not that hungry, are you?"

"I hope he doesn't do that with my gift," said Wynn and I was even more curious.

"Well, give it to him and we'll see," I urged.

Wynn pulled his hand from his tunic and there was the fluffiest, smallest, brightest-eyed little huskie pup I had ever seen.

"Wynn!" I squealed, "how did you keep him so quiet?"

"It wasn't easy."

I reached for the puppy but Samuel beat me to it. I do think that Samuel would have put the puppy into his mouth as well if he had had opportunity, but after holding the puppy close so that Samuel could feel its softness, Wynn took him back and placed him on the floor.

He sat there, blinking his big blue eyes and looking at this strange new place. Kip joined the act then. He had been watching the whole procedure, his head cocked to one side, but now he came forward to sniff at the puppy and see if it really was a dog.

The puppy immediately turned to Kip, rejoicing to see one of its own kind and greeted Kip with such exuberance that Kip backed off and eventually retreated, the puppy tumbling along after him.

We laughed together at the sight.

I turned to Wynn. "How are we ever going to fit another body in this house? We already have three people and a dog."

"He's quite capable of living outside," said Wynn. "He doesn't need to be in the house at all. Every boy needs a dog of his own."

I shook my head. I was sure Wynn already knew that I would never be able to put that puppy outside alone. He would be sharing the fireside rug with Kip.

We had our breakfast then and together prepared for our journey.

I don't know when I ever enjoyed a day so much. Samuel seemed to understand that this great outdoors—this wilderness—was a part of himself. He studied it all with big, black, serious eyes, pointing his finger and chattering about the things that caught his attention.

Both Wynn and I were pleased at the small child's response.

"He's a sharp little fellow, isn't he, Wynn?" I couldn't resist asking.

Wynn agreed.

We ate our birthday dinner on a blanket spread out on the soft floor of the forest, cushioned by years of pine needles. Wynn gave Samuel a large pine cone to play with while I arranged the picnic lunch. As usual, it went to his mouth.

We traveled on to the beaver dam and let Samuel watch the beavers at work, telling him the native word for the small energetic animal. We even pretended that he tried to say the word after us but, to be honest, I think it was just more of his baby gibberish.

We took Samuel down to the pond's edge and Wynn held him so he could splash his hand back and forth in the cool water. His eyes brightened and he splashed so hard that even Wynn was getting wet.

When we took him from the pond he coaxed to go back, pointing and complaining as he was carried away.

The sun was in the west and beginning its descent when we turned toward home. We had not gone far when I noticed that Samuel, on his father's back, was sound asleep, his little dark head nodding with each step Wynn took.

"We've played the poor little fellow out," I said sympathetically.

Wynn chuckled. "I think he's enjoyed every minute of it."

"I think so too. I'm so glad you thought of it, Wynn. It was fun, wasn't it?"

Wynn reached for my hand and we walked home together. Kip ran on ahead, searching out rabbit burrows, or squirrel hide-outs. Samuel slept on. Perhaps his dreams were of wilderness things. He looked contented and healthy.

"We must get home to feed his puppy," I said, and Wynn tightened his grip on my hand.

Two nights later we were sitting by the open fire, Wynn working on some records, I doing some hand sewing and Samuel sleeping in his nearby bed, when there was a sound at our door. Kip rose quickly with a sharp bark, upsetting the puppy who slept beside him.

"Hush, Kip," I commanded, afraid that the barking might waken the baby.

Wynn got up and went to the door, expecting, as I was, someone with a problem.

It was young Joe Henry Running Deer who stood on the doorstep.

It took me awhile to recognize him, but when I did a slow smile crossed my face. He had come to see his son. I was sure he would be pleased to see we had taken good care of him.

Wynn greeted him and motioned him in. He came, rather hesitantly, urging a woman ahead of him. She looked young, hardly more than a girl, and very shy. I wondered if it was his sister.

He did not come farther into the room, did not ask to see his child, but instead pushed the girl forward a bit more and spoke in broken English, "New woman now. I come for son."

The blood drained from my face. I hoped I had misunderstood him. I looked at Wynn. His face was white, too, and I looked back at the young man again, about to ask him what in the world he was talking about. Wynn said something to him and the man answered, but I didn't hear or understand what either of them was saying.

"What is he saying?" I demanded of Wynn. "Why is he here?"

"Stay calm, Elizabeth," Wynn told me. But I couldn't stay calm.

"Wynn," I demanded, "what did he say?"

Wynn turned to me then, his eyes filled with anguish.

"He has come for his child. He wants him back, Elizabeth."

I wanted to scream, to protest, but my throat would let no words come. I looked imploringly at Wynn, begging him with my eyes to get the two of them out of our cabin.

Wynn was still talking softly to the young man. I couldn't hear his words, but surely he was explaining the situation. *Samuel is our baby now! We will not give him up.* Joe Henry and his young bride could have many more children of their own.

I looked at the crib. Samuel was stirring. The noise in the cabin must have disturbed him. I jumped to my feet and rushed to his bed, ready to take him in my arms and shield him. He was still sleeping. I looked up again. Wynn was easing our visitors from the cabin. *Soon this whole nightmare will be over—it has to be!* Wynn closed the door, standing for a few moments with his head leaning against it. There was a droop to his shoulders I had never seen before. I wanted to cross to him, to tell him that it was all right now, but my legs wouldn't work. I sat back down slowly on the cot, and Wynn straightened his shoulders and turned to me.

"We should have been prepared for this, Elizabeth," he said sorrowfully. "We should have known."

"It's all right now," I told him. "I'm sure he understands. After all, it's been almost a year since he gave him to us. He can't just walk in and—"

"Elizabeth," cut in Wynn, "it's his child."

"He gave him to us."

"Not—not the way we thought." Wynn sounded very tired.

"But he's gone now."

"He'll be back."

I was on my feet then, terror bringing the strength back to my legs. "What do you mean? What are you saying?" I demanded. "You sent him away, didn't you?"

There was a defeated look on Wynn's face. "I sent him away, yes, so that we'd have a little time, a little time to think, a little time to prepare ourselves."

"What did you tell him?"

"I don't know. Something—something about the baby being asleep and we didn't want him to lose his dream or something. I'm really not sure. I just said the first thing that came to my mind."

Wynn shrugged his shoulders.

"And he's coming back?" I said in an empty voice.

"In the morning," said Wynn.

"Well, we won't let him go."

"There's no way to stop it, Elizabeth. He wants his baby."

"We'll go to court; we'll fight it."

"And only delay the agony. We wouldn't stand a chance."

I started to cry then—deep, agonizing sobs that shook my whole body. Wynn moved to comfort me, to hold me in his arms, and then I realized that Wynn was weeping, too. I don't suppose anything would have brought me to my senses more quickly. Knowing of Wynn's deep pain brought me out of myself. Wynn needed me. We needed each other. We were losing our baby. In the morning Samuel would be gone and there was nothing we could do about it.

For a moment I hated the young man. How could he do such a thing? And then, I dared to go a step further. I became very angry at God. Why was He letting such a thing happen? I tried to push the anger from me, knowing that it wasn't right, but it would not go away. I clung to Wynn and cried some more.

There was very little sleep for us that night. We talked, we prayed, I cried, but we did not rid ourselves of the deep pain within us.

I arose quietly about three o'clock to go out and check on Samuel. I crept quietly so that I would not waken Wynn, but when I entered the room, Wynn was already there, bending over the small boy, watching him sleep in the semidarkness, the open fire sending shivery little shadows over his face.

I went to Wynn's side and wordlessly took his hand. Again the tears fell. *We loved him so. We had thought him ours. We had planned his future.*

I went to make some coffee. We drank it together silently,

our eyes on the baby. Kip seemed to understand that something was wrong. He came to me and pressed his muzzle into my hand, whimpering deep in his throat.

"We need to talk," said Wynn.

I nodded.

"They'll be here in a few hours."

Still I said nothing.

"What do you want to send with him?"

I couldn't name the things one by one—all the things Wynn and I had made for Samuel. I knew I would send all of them. I wanted him to have familiar things. Besides, they only would be hurtful reminders left with us.

"I'll pack his things," I managed through numb lips, and got up to do so.

I guess I cried over everything I packed. The little clothes, the blankets, the Christmas toys, the gifts that had come. I emptied the drawer where I had kept his things, and then I reached for the little calico horse and wept some more.

"Why, God? Why?" my heart kept crying, but there was no answer.

When I had all of his things packed and my tears under control, I rejoined Wynn by the fire.

"What about the puppy?" I asked Wynn. "We haven't even picked out a name for him yet."

"Samuel should name him. If Joe wants him, he can go."

"And if he doesn't?"

"Jim Buck has always wanted a dog. He can take him if his parents say it's okay."

The sky was beginning to lighten. I knew that Joe and his new wife would soon come. They were traveling to the big village and would want to leave early. I thought I should invite them for breakfast, but I could not bring myself to do so. I went to the bedroom and dressed. Wynn was already in his uniform.

I came out and walked to the crib again, looking down at the sleeping Samuel. "Wynn," I said, "I don't think I want to be here when they come."

Wynn nodded his head in understanding.

"I was wondering," he said slowly, "if you'd like me to take Samuel to them, so they won't need to come here?"

I hesitated, thinking over Wynn's suggestion.

"I—I think so," I agreed.

"Then we'd better get him up and get him fed and ready."

Wynn got the baby up and dressed him while I fixed his morning porridge, and then we gave him his breakfast. We had prayer together, asking God to go with our Samuel, wherever his path led—to keep him, and protect him, and most of all to give him opportunity to know Him as we had planned that he should.

Samuel seemed to think it was just another morning. He squealed at his puppy, chewed on his little horse and grabbed handfuls of Kip's fur. We gathered all his things then and Wynn took the small baby in his arms and the bundle on his back, the puppy tucked within his tunic as he had brought him home such a short time ago, and set off for the village after I had given Samuel one last squeeze.

I wondered as I watched them go with the tears streaming down my cheeks if life would ever again have meaning for me.

Chapter Thirty-three

Sorrow and Joy

The next weeks were the worst days of my life. I wandered in an empty world, void of feeling except for pain. The house was empty, the bed in the corner—which I had insisted remain where it was—was empty, but worst of all, my life was empty as well.

At times I tried to pray but God seemed far away. I knew it wasn't God's fault. He hadn't moved. I had. I no longer felt close to Him. I couldn't understand how He could have let this happen.

I didn't even feel close to Wynn. He quietly went about his daily tasks. I tended to mine. He tried to communicate, to hold me, to get me to talk it out, but I resisted, putting him off with one flimsy excuse or another.

I lost weight, which was not surprising. I wasn't eating. I still couldn't sleep. I just lay in bed at night, wondering what was happening to Samuel.

Nimmie came to see me, and brought her children. Where before I would have enjoyed their play and their laughter, now it was only a cruel reminder; and when Nimmie invited me to her house, I found reasons to stay at home.

There was nothing to do at home. No sewing, little washing, no reason to make special food or plan special childish games. Jim Buck came to see me, wondering when we would

217

be starting classes again; but I put him off with some evasive answer and told him that I would bang on the drum when I was ready for classes to resume.

I took in my garden and stored the vegetables—not because I found pleasure in it, but because it was something to do. Almost daily I went for long walks with Kip. I didn't enjoy the walking, but it got me away from the village and I would not need to try to act civil to other people.

I knew Wynn was worried about me, but I really couldn't make myself care.

When winter's snow swept in, burying all the uncleanness of the village beneath a blanket of white, I watched without comment. *It would be nice*, I thought, *to be able to bury one's feelings as completely.*

But God had not forgotten me. Day by day snatches of scripture verses began to chip away at the coldness of my heart. Little phrases and promises began to come to my mind. There were those who prayed, I know, and perhaps it was in response to them that the Lord kept working with me. It was also because I was His child and He loved me.

One day as I looked at the snow lying cold and clean on the village paths, I thought of the verse, "Wash me, and I shall be whiter than snow." For some reason I got a look at my heart as the words flashed before me. In the past I had been washed, I had been cleansed. I had then bowed before my Maker with a guilt-free conscience because of the washing, cleansing power of His blood. I didn't feel clean now. I felt defiled. Dirty. Angry and bitter. I knew that if I bowed before Him now, it could be only with a head hung down in shame.

"But it's your fault, God," I condemned Him. "Look at the pain you caused me."

"He was wounded for our transgressions, he was bruised for our iniquities," whispered in my mind.

"I know, I know," I admitted reluctantly. "You did send your Son to die for me. It did cause you pain. I've said I'm sorry. I've asked for forgiveness for my sin, but this is something different. As your child I thought you would shield me, care for me—but here I am. I'm all alone and I'm hurting, Lord—because you—"

"For the Lord your God is a merciful God; he will not forsake you or destroy you," came the scripture verse.

"But I feel forsaken, Lord. I feel empty and—"

"Call on me, and I will answer you, and show you great and mighty things, which you do not know."

"Could you, Lord? Could you really help me? Could you lift this burden from my heart and make life meaningful again?"

"For you shall go out with joy, and be led out with peace; the mountains and the hills shall break forth into singing before you, and all the trees of the field shall clap their hands."

That was what I needed, what I longed for. Perhaps it wasn't the absence of Samuel that was making my life so miserable, but the absence of the presence of God. *I must find that joy again. I must.* I took my Bible and went to my bedroom. I would spend as long on my knees as necessary to find and restore the peace with Him that I had known.

I had to go right back to the beginning and work my way through God's plan for mankind. I knew that in order to have peace with God one must meet His conditions. The first thing I had to do was to confess my sin. In this case it was my bitterness and resentment. I was angry with God because I had not borne a child. I was angry with God for taking from me the children I had learned to love, first Susie and then baby Samuel. I had no right to blame God. He couldn't be held accountable for Susie's family's decision to move, or for Joe Henry's choice to come for his son. And how did I know but that those actions might not be for the best? What I *did* know was that God was in charge of my life. He was my sovereign God. He knew what was good for me, and I needed to understand that in His great love for me, He would comfort and sustain me through this devastating loss. *He will give me what is best*, I determined.

I cried out in repentance, and all of the bitterness began to melt from my soul. I then went on to tell God that I accepted His plan for my life, whatever it was, even if it meant I would be childless, and I would stop fighting against it and leave things in His hands. I no longer wanted to be miserable or to bring misery to others. I thought of Wynn and the pain I had caused him. I asked the Lord to forgive me, and vowed to ask Wynn to forgive me also.

I prayed for Samuel. I prayed also for Joe Henry Running Deer, that he would be a good and wise father. That somehow Joe might be given opportunity to know the Lord so that he could introduce Samuel, and any more sons and daughters that he might be blessed with, to the Savior.

I prayed for the young girl who was now Samuel's mother. I prayed that God would help her in her motherhood. That she would be loving and kind, patient and caring, and that she would grow to love Samuel as I had loved him.

I talked to God about many things, keeping nothing back, and by the time I rose from my knees I felt clean and at peace again.

I knew there still would be days ahead when I might wish for a child. I would take those days as they came, asking God to help me through them, but I was sure that I would not chafe and be impatient and insistent. With God's help I would look for the joy in life that He would choose to give me. It was foolish to go through life pouting and complaining and making myself miserable when I already had so much to be thankful for. I would make each day an experience with the Lord. I would find many things to thank Him for. I started out by thanking Him for Wynn.

Wynn knew as soon as he came in our door that something had happened. I shared my experience with him that night. We spent some time talking it over and praying together. It was good to feel whole and close again. "I shouldn't have acted as I did," I admitted. "I will treasure the memories of the days spent with Samuel. They will always be special to me."

We removed the crib from the living quarters. We no longer needed those kinds of painful reminders. We had pleasant memories now, and we found that we could share them together. "Remember when?" one of us would say, and we would both laugh at the incident.

We cherished the pictures Wawasee had made. Many of them I mounted and hung in our bedroom. Each day as I looked at them, I thanked God again for giving us those precious months of parenting Samuel.

Wynn entered the cabin with a strange-looking document in his hands.

"What's that?" I asked.

"A new posting," was his reply.

"A new posting—how did you get that?"

"A special runner just brought it."

"Can't we just stay on here?" I asked, frowning as I thought of all of our friends in the village.

"The Force feels that it is not wise to leave a man for too long in one area."

"Why?"

"There is the chance of becoming too attached to certain friends, or making enemies."

"So where is it? Still in the North?" I asked, coming closer to get a look at the paper.

"It is, but it really doesn't matter," Wynn said rather absently. "I'm not going to take it."

"You're not?" I was surprised. Wynn usually did not question his orders. "How do you get out of it?"

"Request it. Under the circumstances, I think they will be reasonable."

Wynn took the paper to his office and then came back out. He kissed me and turned to go. "We'll talk about it later," he said.

I did a lot of thinking after he had gone. Somehow I knew

it was because of me that Wynn was thinking of questioning the order. I looked down at myself. I was still skinny, but I was eating better now. I was sure that in no time I would be up to the proper weight again. I was sleeping fine now, too, and I had resumed classes and was having ladies in for tea and getting out to the village. I was enjoying life again, and I was wise enough to know that when we left this village, I would be lonesome for the friends we had made. And the thought of leaving dear Nimmie brought a special pang of sorrow.

But I was no longer afraid, nor was I bitter. I was now willing to walk in God's path for my life. With Him it did not matter where one lived or the circumstances of the living. Wherever one was located, there could still be peace and joy.

I did not bring up the matter of the letter. We had settled before our fire that evening when Wynn spoke.

"You wondered about that new posting," he said, lowering the book he was reading. "It was to Smoke Lake."

"Where's Smoke Lake?"

"North and west of us."

"Bigger or smaller?" I asked.

"A little bigger, I guess."

"What's it like?"

"It's even more primitive than it is here."

There was silence for several minutes.

"You've decided not to take it because of me, right?"

Wynn hedged. "Well, not because I think you couldn't handle it, only because I don't think it would be fair to you."

"Why?"

"As I said, it's even more difficult and secluded than it is here."

"What will you do then?"

Wynn had laid aside his book and was giving me his complete attention. "I will ask for a post back in civilization. If not Calgary or Edmonton, at least a fair-sized town where you can live similar to the way you are used to living, Elizabeth. The North has been hard on you. You've been asked to give so much, and you've always been willing, but it's time now—"

I did not let Wynn finish. "You know," I said, "it was good for me to make that trip to Calgary. I found out that stores and sidewalks and even bathrooms aren't necessary for life after all."

"You're saying that you don't want to go back?" Wynn asked incredulously.

"No, I'm not saying that. I could enjoy living back there, too. But I don't need it to be happy. I can be happy here just as well. Don't you see, Wynn, the important thing is being with you."

"But I'd be with you."

"In body maybe, but your heart would still be in the North. I wouldn't want that, Wynn, and I don't think either of us would be happy under those circumstances."

There was silence again.

"So just what are you saying?" Wynn finally asked.

I stood up and walked to the fire. I threw on another log and watched the sparks fly upward, reminding me of the multitude of stars in the clear northern sky over our cabin.

"I'm saying, let's take that posting, now, while we are young and healthy and want to do it. There will be plenty of time for city living in the years ahead. The people need us, Wynn. There are lots of men and their wives who are willing to take the city postings. We're needed here." I hesitated for a moment. "Who knows what exciting things might be just over the next hill?"

Wynn stood to his feet and took me in his arms. He looked deeply into my eyes. "You're sure?" he asked me.

"Perfectly sure."

And I was. With Wynn's arms about me and God's peace in my heart, I had no reason to doubt or fear anything the future might hold.